WHAT MONSTER?

By Liz Pichon

Scholastic Canada Ltd.

Scholastic Canada Ltd.
604 King Street West, Toronto, Ontario M5V 1E1, Canada

Scholastic Inc.
557 Broadway, New York, NY 10012, USA

Scholastic Australia Pty Limited
PO Box 579, Gosford, NSW 2250, Australia

Scholastic New Zealand Limited
Private Bag 94407, Botany, Manukau 2163, New Zealand

Scholastic Children's Books
Euston House, 24 Eversholt Street, London NW1 1DB, UK

www.scholastic.ca

Library and Archives Canada Cataloguing in Publication

Pichon, Liz, author, illustrator
What monster? / Liz Pichon.

(Tom Gates)
ISBN 978-1-4431-7558-6 (softcover)

I. Title. II. Series: Pichon, Liz. Tom Gates.

j823'.92   C2018-906663-6

PZ7.P53Wh 2019

First published in the UK by Scholastic Ltd., 2018.

6 5 4 3 2 1   Printed in Canada 139   19 20 21 22 23

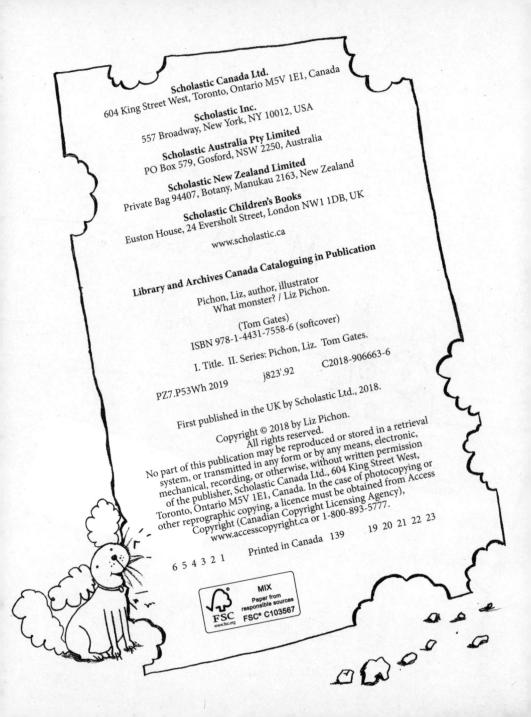

MIX
Paper from
responsible sources
FSC® C103567

OAKFIELD GAZETTE

AUTHOR
dedicates BOOK
to ACE reader
Zach and TOP
merch stall
seller Lysette
XX

Mr Fullerman is standing RIGHT in front of me and saying the word NEW a lot.

We have a **NEW** school play ... blah blah ... and a **NEW** teacher ... blah blah... Who needs a **NEW** worksheet?

(Not me – I haven't finished THIS one yet.)

I put on my BEST "I'm concentrating" face so it looks like I'm working. BUT really I'm thinking about all the different things that HAPPENED this morning...

Sigh...

(It's hard NOT to ... and here's WHY. ➡)

Derek and I were on our way to school when we SPOTTED a funny sign outside the shop.

It was for the local **NEWSPAPER** and the headline said:

Which made us LAUGH!

OAKFIELD GAZETTE

ANGRY SQUIRREL THROWS NUTS!

I wonder what made the squirrel SO ANGRY in the first place? Grrrrr

I said.

Maybe the squirrel had a spelling test that didn't go well, so it had a HUGE squirrel meltdown and threw nuts EVERYWHERE,

Derek told me in a really serious voice, which made it sound even funnier.

"Do squirrels have spelling tests?"
I wondered.

"They might do – you never know,"
Derek said, like that explained EVERYTHING.
Then I thought of something else that could have
happened.

"Maybe the squirrel's got an annoying
sister who keeps pinching all
the best acorns and driving it **CRAZY!**"
(If my sister Delia was a squirrel, that's
exactly what she'd do to me.)

Mine

Hey!

Whatever...

We decided to go into the shop and take
a sneaky read of the **NEWSPAPER**
to find out what really happened.

"Have we got enough time?"
Derek asked.
I looked at my digital watch.

Tons.

(Ten minutes, to be precise. I thought we'd be OK.)

The trouble was a lady had put her bag right on top of the **newspapers**, which meant we couldn't read ANYTHING.

"That's annoying," I muttered.

"There's more papers over there," Derek whispered and pointed to a small stack in the corner. We snuck over for a quick read, trying to avoid the shopkeeper, who doesn't like it when we LO O K but don't buy anything.

I'd only just picked the paper up when, out of the corner of my EYE, I saw something running towards us.

"Derek! Derek! LOOK! LOOK!"

I shouted excitedly because it was only one of my favourite dogs EVER - a SAUSAGE DOG!

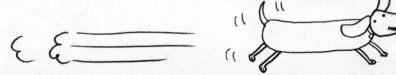

We forgot all about the
ANGRY squirrel story
and sat down to play with the dog instead.

"I wish I had a dog like this," I sighed.
As we were patting its head, a lady came
to join us.

 "Is this your dog?" Derek asked her.

"Yes, he's mine. He's very friendly,"
the lady said. "Do you both go to Oakfield School?"

"Yup. What's your dog's name?"
I asked, as that was a MUCH more
important question.

"His name's Bandit. I'm worried you two
will be late for school if you don't hurry up."

"Nah, we'll be fine. Besides, I've discovered a *sneaky* way into school through the dinner hall that avoids the teachers who hand out the late marks."

I kept patting **Bandit**, who seemed to be enjoying himself.

"A secret entrance, that's good to know. Who's your teacher then, boys?"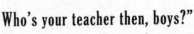

The lady was asking a LOT of questions, but I didn't mind as I got more time with **Bandit**.

"My teacher's Mr Fullerman and Derek's is Mr Sprocket," I replied. "Mr Fullerman's got these BIG beady eyes and he sees EVERYTHING. Well, maybe not everything. He didn't notice me doodling the other day or when I pretended to do a ...

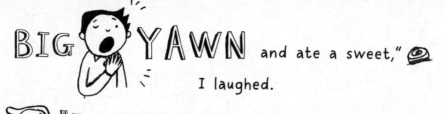 BIG YAWN and ate a sweet," I laughed.

 "I do that **too!** It works well if you do a FAKE *SNEEZE* like this," Derek said while demonstrating.

"Hey, Tom – we'd better go now or we really will be late," he added.

"Awwwwww! I want to stroke **Bandit** some more!"

 "Sorry, boys, I need to get going as well, but I enjoyed our chat. It was VERY interesting and informative," the lady said.

I gave **Bandit** a few more PATS as they both left the shop.

See you again soon, I **hope!**

Derek said and waved.

You will! the lady called back.

I meant the dog, but I suppose we'll probably see that lady too,

Derek told me.

OK, boys, are you BUYING anything or just looking?

the shopkeeper asked us, so we made a quick *exit* and ran all the way to school. We managed to

avoid getting a late mark from

Mr Sprocket by sneaking in

through our secret dinner hall door. Then

Derek went to his class and I nipped

into mine.

Ding Ding

AMY and Marcus were already there, and Marcus looked even MORE MISERABLE than usual.

On a scale of 1 ——— to ——→ 10 his FACE was about ▮▮▮▮▮▮▮▮▮▮▮▮▮▮▮▮▮▮▮ ——→ 11.

FURIOUS

"Hi, Marcus. You look happy. ☺ What's up?" I asked him cheerily, trying to make an effort.

"Haven't you heard what's happening?" he said.

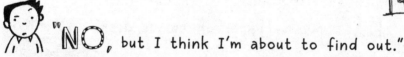

"NO, but I think I'm about to find out."

"Mr Fullerman's going away on some kind of big teacher conference and he's got a TON of work for us all. This isn't going to be a fun week, I can tell."

"**W**ho's taking over?" I asked.

"I don't know," Marcus grumbled.

"We're getting a supply teacher," **AMY** told me.

"**GREAT!** Supply teachers always let you do things that **Mr Fullerman** wouldn't. We'll have nice, **EASY** lessons for sure!" I said confidently.

"There's been rumours..." **AMY** started to say when **Mr Fullerman** plonked another **BIG** pile of paper on to his desk. **THUMP**

"**SEE?** I told you.

ALL those worksheets are for us," Marcus sighed.

"**M**y friend from Blue Coat School told me something interesting," **AMY** whispered.

Marcus *LEANED* over so he could hear what we were talking about.

"She told me the supply teacher from their school is coming to OUR school and she's STRICT."

How strict?

I wanted to know.

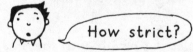
"**VERY**-like, **SUPER STRICT.**"

Awwwwww noooooo,

Marcus moaned.

I was still in a good mood from meeting Bandit, so I tried to look on the BRIGHT side.

"I'm sure she won't be **THAT** bad.

We've had supply teachers before that have let

us do  things – remember?"

Yes, sir – we are allowed to eat sweets
in class and watch films too. It's called
NO WORK WEDNESDAYS.

Then **AMY** told me some more about the

teacher that didn't sound very promising.

"The teacher's name is **M**iss **G**ravel and she has

NO sense of humour **AT ALL**."

"Miss **GRAVVELLL?** Even her name sounds

strict."

Marcus had been EARWIGGING our

conversation and decided that this

was **BIG NEWS**...

... and needed to be shared with the **WHOLE** class.

He told Solid first.

"Pssssst! We've got a new supply teacher and she's called **M**iss **G**ravel – PASS IT ON."

Then Solid told Mark Clump...

"**Hey,** we've got a new supply teacher and she's called Miss Paddle – pass it on..."

Who told Pansy Bennet...

"We've got a new supply teacher who likes to travel – pass it on."

And she told Julia Morton...

"We've got a new supply of T-shirts and they're kind of yellow."

"Why are you whispering?" Julia asks.

"I don't know." Then Julia whispered the news to ...

Brad Galloway

He managed to tell EVERYONE around him EXACTLY what he'd heard.

Blah Blah Blah

Blah Blah Blah

Blah Blah Blah

Bla

Blah!

Brad walked past my desk and wanted to tell ME the NEWS too.

"Hey Tom, have you heard..."

"About the new supply teacher?" I said.

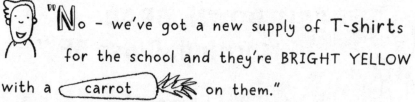 **"N**o - we've got a new supply of T-shirts for the school and they're BRIGHT YELLOW with a carrot on them."

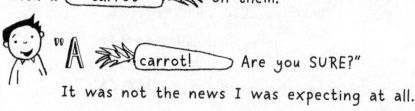 **"A** carrot! Are you SURE?"

It was not the news I was expecting at all.

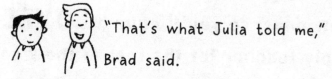 "That's what Julia told me," Brad said.

I was trying to work out why we would have a carrot on a school T-shirt ...

... when **Mr Fullerman** started to tap his desk with his pen.

"SIT DOWN, BRAD.
Morning, Class 5F."

"Morning, Mr Fullerman,"
we replied *slowly.*

"I'm going away on a **very** important teacher conference for a few days, so you'll have a **LOVELY** supply teacher for the rest of the week. I know you're going to be well behaved and do **ALL** your work – won't you?"

"Errrrrrrrrrrrrr, mmmmm, sir," we mumbled
(in a not-very-convincing way).

Marcus kept *nudging* me and saying, "Told you! See? I TOLD you!" as if I hadn't believed him.

"Your NEW teacher is going to LOVE being at Oakfield School."

"Sir, is that PILE of worksheets ALL for us?" Norman asked.

"OF COURSE it is! But don't panic, they're not ALL worksheets."

(Mr Fullerman seemed to be enjoying himself.)

Then AMY put up her hand.

"Sir, what's the new teacher called?"

In my head I was saying...

Not Miss Gravel, not Miss Gravel, not Miss Gravel.

 Mr Fullerman started to say...

**"Hmm. It's Miss... Miss... Miss...
No, sorry, it's gone."**

Brad Galloway called out from the back of the class,

"Is that her NAME, sir?"

Which made the class LAUGH. "Miss Gone!"
he added, in case we didn't get the joke.

**"Very funny, Brad. I believe your
new teacher is coming in to school
today, so I'll check her name and tell you
all later."**

(I was just happy he didn't say Miss Gravel.)

"Imagine if we had a teacher called Miss Take,"
I said to AMY. We spent the next five minutes
thinking of other funny
names for teachers.

Miss Understood.

Miss Out, Miss Heard.

Miss Isle, Miss Spent.

Miss Rable.

Miss Shapen.

Miss Chief.

Miss Strict,

Marcus added, not quite getting the joke.

"And DON'T forget the NEW SCHOOL PLAY AUDITIONS,"

Mr Fullerman reminded us.

"I'm sure the play's going to be a GREAT success, because you're ALL SO TALENTED!"

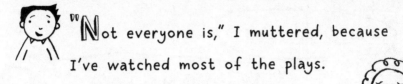 "**N**ot everyone is," I muttered, because
I've watched most of the plays.

I'm going to audition for the LEAD role,"
Marcus told me, sounding very sure of himself.

 "You don't know what it is yet - it could be
a MUSICAL and then you'll have to
do a DANCE or Sing something at the
audition," I pointed out.

"I know - but THAT doesn't worry
me because I am what you call ...

Marcus said confidently.

AMY raised her eyebrows like she was surprised.

"What's **a triple threat?**" I asked him.

"It means I can **SING, DANCE** and **ACT** — see? Triple threat, that's **me.**"

"Sounds more like some kind of an ice cream. I'd like a **TRIPLE THREAT** please with **EXTRA** sprinkles," I told him, which made **AMY** laugh.

"**V**ery FUNNY. I was **SO** good in the last play, I'm sure I'll get a **BIGGER** role this time.

What part did you have again, Tom?" he added.

"**O**h, I can't remember..." I said.

(I did remember – I just didn't want to tell him.)

"Were you a villager in the crowd? **O**r **A** **T**REE! No one wants to be a tree, do they? Being covered in leaves, waving your arms around and **SWAYING** in the pretend WIND."

Marcus kept going on and **ON** about being a **T**REE, saying it was the worst part in a play to get and how boring it must be, when **AMY** interrupted him.

I'm a tree!

"What's wrong with being a TREE? Tom was a very good TREE in the last school play, weren't you?"

(AMY remembers EVERYTHING.)

"Thanks, AMY – I'd forgotten about that," I sighed.

"Was your acting a bit ... WOODEN?" Marcus asked me, laughing at his own joke.

"Actually, Marcus, everyone thought I was TREEmendous," I said right back at him. Marcus groaned.

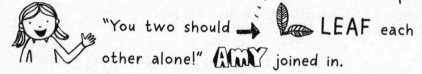

"You two should ➜ LEAF each other alone!" AMY joined in.

"Good one," I said, and we tried to think of more tree jokes.

Nnone of us could, so we moved on.

Annoyingly, Marcus decided to tell me what part I should go for in the school play, even though none of us knew what it was yet.

"You'd be a good narrator, or maybe even an animal - a FUNNY animal."

"Thanks, Marcus, that means a lot to me," I said, not being serious.

"You do realize that not everyone gets a part in the play even when they audition," AMY reminded us, sensibly.

"That won't happen to me – triple threat, remember?"

Marcus replied.

"Just in case, I can give you some good tips on how to be a tree," I LAUGHED.

"Actually, Tom, I'm getting on with my work now if you don't mind?" he told me and looked down at his desk like I was disturbing him.

I decided that I should probably do the same thing and get on with my work as well ...

... right after I finished my
impressive doodle.

Sprinkles

TRIPLE THREAT

AMY glanced over and said,

"That's funny, Tom!" 🙂

For some reason Marcus wasn't quite so keen. 🙁

(I can't think why.)

Marcus wasn't the only person in a slightly **bad** mood. 😕

Caretaker Stan was cross that SOMEONE had dropped food and crumbs all over the corridor floor.

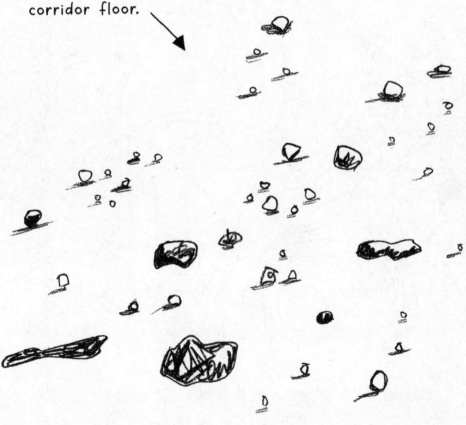

When the bell went for break time, we could hear him saying,

"Who's been dropping food everywhere?"

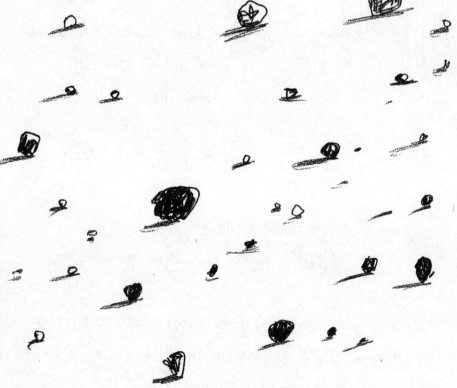

As we walked past him on the way out to break, he said, "Do you know who did this? ANYONE?"

We all kept quiet.

"It must be Mr Nobody again," he sighed, which is something my mum says as well.

Mr Nobody again?

The food trail went right down the hall and into the school grounds.

"At least the birds are helping to clean up." AMY pointed at them pecking up the crumbs.

While everyone was watching the birds, I suggested that it could be a good time to go and play a game of CHAMP while the square was FREE.

"Good thinking!" Derek said as we raced each other over to the square and everyone followed. But when we got there ... it wasn't FREE. The little kids were already playing on it.

"How did that happen?" Solid said.

"Shall we just wait for them to finish?" I wondered. Norman reminded us how good they all were at Champ. "See what I mean?"

It was getting a bit boring looking at them hitting the ball to one another and not being out.

"**A**re you lot going to be much longer?"
Mark Clump asked.

"Yes. We were here first, remember?"
the kid in the first CHAMP square told us.
Which was true, but also quite annoying.

Before we gave up, I remembered
something I had in my pocket.

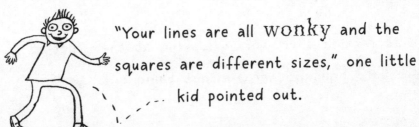

I've got
EMERGENCY CHALK!

It was only a small piece, but enough to draw out
another square for us to play in.

"Your lines are all wonky and the
squares are different sizes," one little
kid pointed out.

"Oh well, the ground's **rougher** here, that's all,"
I said like it wasn't important.

4 | 1
3 | 2

Florence went and got us a ball from the
playground equipment box, but it looked like it
had been CHEWED UP.
"Sorry, it's the only
one I could find."

CLOSE UP

"It's better than nothing," I told her.

"Only just..." **AMY** said, trying to make it bounce.

The ball kept .... going off in

all different directions ...

4 1
3 2

... which made our game of CHAMP very
tricky and the little kids kept laughing at us.

You do know you're supposed to HIT the ball, don't you?

one Champ girl said.

"It's not our fault – it's the BALL. It keeps going WONKY,"

I pointed out.

"This is impossible. How can we play with this stupid thing?" Marcus grumbled. He was still waiting for his turn, as we weren't moving round very fast.

"You lot just can't play CHAMP, that's all," the Champ girl told us.

"Well, OK – let's SWAP the balls then and see if you can play with OUR one," Marcus suggested.

Before the little kids could say anything, Marcus swapped their ball for the manky one.

"HEY!" the Champ girl called out.

"You said the ball doesn't make a difference, so LET'S SEE," he told them.

"OK — WATCH THIS," the Champ girl said.

Then they carried on playing ...

like there was

nothing

wrong with

the ball at all.

4 1
3 2

(They were THAT good at CHAMP.)

(See page 232 for RULES of CHAMP, in case you don't know.)

Marcus was SO keen to get <u>OUR</u> game going,
he jumped into the CHAMP square and said,
"Let's SHOW these kids what WE can do!"
He threw the ball HIGH up into the air, spun round,
and completely lost his balance. Then he HIT the
ball really HARD ...

... in completely the WRONG direction.

The ball flew over our heads and landed on the
other side of the school grounds.

Oh...

Whack!

Marcus looked DIZZY from all the spinning, and then he stumbled into the little kids' game and HIT their ball too!

"What did you do that for?"

a little boy shouted.

"I got confused. I couldn't focus," Marcus said.

"Brilliant," I sighed. Now no one could play CHAMP. The little kids asked for my piece of CHALK so they could play hopscotch instead while we went to try and find both the balls. ☹

"They landed over there," AMY said, pointing to the other side of the school grounds.

"Well, this is a BIG waste of my break time," Marcus muttered as he reluctantly came to help us look.

"Are you sure they landed here?" Florence asked, as we couldn't see either of them.

"I think so," I said, and we all kept searching right up until the bell went for the end of break.

"Maybe someone's put the balls back in the equipment box already?" Florence wondered.

"They're probably right HERE under our noses and we just can't see them," AMY said, peering into the plants.

"It's pointless - let's go," Marcus grumbled, not being helpful at all.

Trying to get back to class wasn't easy either. There was a BIG hold-up in the corridor, which turned out to be the little kids all crowded round the poster about the NEW school play.

None of us could see it properly. "What's the play?" AMY asked, but no one answered.

We could hear **Buster Jones** stomping down the corridor telling everyone:

Buster takes his corridor monitor job very seriously. He waved all the kids on and then STOOD in the way so we STILL couldn't see what it was.

NEW SCHOOL
PLAY
a...ns

"**BUSTER!** What's the school PLAY this year?" I asked, pointing at the poster.

"Oh," he said, and turned around (still blocking our view). Then he told us,

It's **Star Wars.**

NEW SCHOOL
PLAY
a...ns

"**Star Wars** for a school play? We've never done anything like THAT before."

"Ambitious..." **AMY** said.

We all started to imagine the fun we'd have with lightsabers when **Buster** said ...

"Sorry, I'm reading the wrong thing.
It's actually JACK AND THE BEANSTALK."

 "Shame," I said, slightly disappointed.
"I could have been a **WOOKIE**," Solid
told us, then did a very good impression.

Aaawwh!

Which was alarming, but very convincing.

Marcus seemed **E**XTRA pleased with the choice

of play and told us,

> Well, I think we ALL
> know what part I'll be
> going for NOW.

 "The beanstalk?" I suggested.

"Of COURSE not," he said crossly.

"How about the golden goose?"

(Goose)

"I can see you as the goose!" I added.

Don't be ridiculous.

I want

to be ... THE GIANT.

"I thought you were going to say you wanted to be Jack," Norman told him. (We all did.)

No - the GIANT will be far more FUN to play,

Marcus said, then added,

"Besides, I can't think of anyone else who'd make a better GIANT than me. Can you?"

(I wasn't sure if he was joking or not.)

45

Solid put up his hand and said,

"I CAN!"

(I think Marcus forgot about Solid.)

Mr Fullerman is smiling at us as we sit back down (which is a good sign – I think?). He says we can choose what we want to do until lunchtime. Brad asks if he can do Nothing?

"What do you think, Brad? And before you ask, sleeping isn't an option either," Mr Fullerman tells him.

AMY starts reading her book and Marcus carries on with his worksheet while still thinking about what part he might play if he doesn't get to be the GIANT. (He won't.)

I'm finishing off my doodle (and the worksheet, officially) when something catches my EYE out of the window.

It's a cardboard box that's moving on its own! I lean back to watch it, when Mr Fullerman tells me to sit straight.

Mr Fullerman doesn't seem that interested in the box and tells me to FOCUS on my work.

"YES, SIR," I say, and then do a quick side glance out of the window to check where the box is now...

It's MOVED AGAIN.

"SIR! THE BOX! THE BOX! It's MOVING!"

I say a bit loudly. Lots of kids stand up to have a look but Mr Fullerman is having none of it.

SIT DOWN!

"TOM, you'll be moving next to ME if you don't get on with some work!"

"But, sir..." I mutter, and wait until he's not looking

before whispering to **AMY**,

"The box really was moving."

"Maybe the WIND blew it forward, Tom.

I don't want to get in trouble with **Mr Fullerman**.

I'm reading," she says and turns a page

of her book.

Marcus, on the other hand, thinks it's FUNNY

to stir things up.

"Psssst, Tom! I know why it's moving."

 "Really?" I say.

"Yes, it's a MAGIC box

that's got wings, OBVIOUSLY!"

he LAUGHs.

"I'm not making it up!" I say, but Marcus starts talking about FOOD.

"Anyway, I can't wait for lunch because I've got the BEST sausage roll EVER. Yum! Do you like sausage rolls, Tom?" he wants to know.

 "Yes, but I'm not thinking about lunch yet – I'm looking at the box ."

"Mmmmmmm... Mmmmm... Sausage rolls..." he keeps saying.

 "Ok, Marcus, I get it," I sigh.

"I can't WAIT to BITE into my DELICIOUS sausage roll!"

He starts pretending to eat one now.

It's hard to concentrate while he's making all those NOISES. "Mmmmm. Mmmmmm."

I take ANOTHER sneaky PEEK out of the window and I can still see the box SHUFFLING along the ground.

"Can you see THAT, Marcus? QUICK, LOOK!" I say, trying to get his attention.

"You're in the way, Tom," Marcus tells me.

"Thank you, TOM and Marcus, for agreeing to stay behind and tidy up."

BUT, SIR! we both say.

Mr Fullerman doesn't want to hear ANY excuses.

"Shhhhhh ... enough chit-chat,"

he tells us sternly.

"See me after the bell goes, you two."

Marcus is NOT happy at all.

"Thanks a LOT, Tom. I'll have to wait even

longer to eat my sausage roll NOW,"

he whispers grumpily.

"It wasn't MY fault," I whisper back.

I STILL think there's something ODD going on with

the box outside.

We sit quietly and get

on with our work until the bell goes.

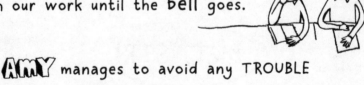

 AMY manages to avoid any TROUBLE

(as usual).

Mr Fullerman makes us collect all the pens and papers up, then push all the chairs under the tables – QUIETLY.

SCRRRAAAPPE
SCRRAAPE
SCRRAAPE

Which takes a while.

"Right, you two – more concentration in the afternoon, OK?"

Yes, sir, we both say then BOLT as FAST as we can to get our packed lunches.

Every class has its own set of shelves on wheels that gets left near the dinner hall so you can collect your food on the way in.

But today there's a problem.

A few kids can't find their lunch boxes, and some are even OPEN.

One kid is complaining,

My food's gone!

Mrs Worthington is trying to sort things out.

Marcus starts to  PANIC until he sees his lunch is safe.

Phew

It's chewed!

My sandwich is half eaten.

Mine's still there too, which is a relief. ☺

"I wonder what's going on?" I ask Marcus, who's not interested and just wants to EAT his sausage roll.

Who cares?

We find a seat next to Derek, who's not sitting in our usual spot.

"The little CHAMP kids were sitting there," he tells me.

"They get everywhere before us, don't they?" I say and open my lunch box.

Delia's left me a NOTE inside, which is nice of her (NOT).

"You should add your own doodle and give it back to her," Derek suggests.

It's a good idea and it doesn't take long.

Favourite Child

That's me.

(Sorry, Tom)

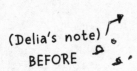

(Delia's note)
BEFORE

STUPID

Favourite Child

That's me.

I'm a twit

AFTER

(Sorry, Tom)

HA! HA!

I tell Derek about the *MOVING* box and he also thinks it could have been a gust of ~WIND pushing it along.

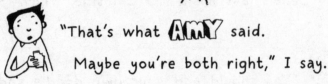

"That's what AMY said.

Maybe you're both right," I say.

I'm agreeing with Derek when Marcus begins to SHOUT,

"WHERE'S MY SAUSAGE ROLL?!"

He empties his lunch box all over the table, but can't find it anywhere.

"NO! NO! Who's taken my sausage ROLL?"

"He's been going on about that SAUSAGE ROLL all morning," I tell Derek. AGH!

Julia Morton asks Marcus if he's got the right lunch box. "There was a LOT of confusion today."

"It's MINE and I DEFINITELY put a sausage roll inside. Someone's PINCHED my food!"

"Why would someone do that?" I ask him.

"BECAUSE it was only the BEST SAUSAGE ROLL EVER!"

"We'll just HAVE to take your word for it now," I tell him and then I offer round my carrot sticks as I've got too many.

Carrot stick, anyone?

Mark Clump takes one then joins in the chat as he's got his own ideas about what happened to the SAUSAGE ROLL.

"I've been thinking about the missing FOOD. You could have dropped it on the way to school then something ATE it, like a fox or a BEAR."

(Mark Clump has a way of telling stories that makes everyone listen.)

"I didn't drop it – someone TOOK it!"
Marcus tells him.

"I'm just saying it's POSSIBLE, that's all.
Whatever took your food might have the
TASTE for it now – and want MORE."

"What does THAT mean?"
Julia Morton wants to know. (We all do.)

"Well, if it was a creature it'll probably be
BACK looking for other things to eat, like..."

LOOK, FOOD!

YUM!

 # SAUSAGE ROLLS!

Norman shouts out.

"Whoever pinched it better NOT try again!"

Marcus says, getting cross.

"Do you remember the time someone found a SNAKE in their toilet? It was in the papers and everything!" Mark reminds us. **I DO!**

NEWSPAPER HEADLINE ➡

OAKFIELD GAZETTE
SNEAKY SNAKE FOUND IN TOILET

 "How did a snake end up in a toilet?" Julia Morton wants to know.

"Sometimes animals **ESCAPE** from their owners, or they get too **BIG** and they're LET LOOSE in the **WILD.** That's what happened to the snake. It hid in some pipes and popped up ...

... in a **toilet**."

Hello!

Mark keeps freaking everyone out with
his creature stories.

"That's like the BIG CAT that was
SPOTTED over the FIELDS.
It's supposed to have escaped from a zoo years
ago and comes out to look for food..."

SAUSAGE ROLLS,

Norman shouts again.

"EXACTLY! That's my point. It could be
anything sneaking around searching for its LUNCH!"

"I hope not," I say,
then offer round my carrot sticks again.

"I don't think an ANIMAL stole my sausage
roll. It was someone in this SCHOOL.
That's why I have a PLAN."

61

"I'm going to set a TRAP!" Marcus tells us dramatically.

"What kind of trap?" I ask.

"It's not going to HURT anyone or ANYTHING, is it? Like a BEAR or a BIG CAT?" Roar

 Mark Clump adds.

"No, of course NOT. Though I can't tell you what it is YET, because it's a **SECRET**," Marcus says.

"You should call it **Operation Sausage Roll**," Derek suggests, which makes everyone laugh (apart from Marcus).

"I'm HUNGRY. I'm eating my sandwich before THAT goes missing too," he tells us.

(It won't.)

While we're finishing our lunches, I spot the little kids are still here too. THIS would be a good time to go and play CHAMP, I'm thinking.

 "Come on, Marcus – let's go and have a PROPER game of Champ. It'll take your mind off your sausage roll," I suggest.

 "I doubt it..." he grumbles, but he comes anyway, along with everyone who played last time.

"If we hurry we'll get to the CHAMP SQUARE first and can play for as long as we want," I say.

(Or that's what I thought.)

SOMEHOW...

the little kids have beaten us to the square AGAIN.

 "How have they done THAT?" I want to know.

"They weren't distracted by SAUSAGE ROLLS," Derek points out.

"We're off to do something else then," AMY tells us.

"Me too. I'm going to LOOK out for any suspicious goings-on around the school and work on my PLAN!" Marcus says.

Which reminds me about the ≡MOVING cardboard box . I ask Derek if he wants to try and find it with me.

"Caretaker Stan has probably taken it away by now — don't you think?" he says.

"Maybe, I'm not sure," I say.

"So what do you want to do instead?" I ask Derek, who takes out from his pocket a whole PACK of CHALK!

 "Look what I brought with me!" he says.

(Derek is a GENIUS.)

"CHALK'S always useful!" he tells me.

Which is true.  Yeah!

We find a good spot to draw on the ground, then INVENT a NEW game called ➤

WHAT MONSTER?

You play it like THIS:

I tell Derek what to draw...

A big **ROUND** body...
- covered in HAIR,
- with two HUGE, WIGGLY EYES on the top of its head,
- wearing a top hat,
- with wings,
- a cheesy smile, with missing teeth,
- a cat tail with spikes,
- and two spider legs wearing flippers.

And this is what he draws!

(Excellent monster.)

Now it's **D**erek's turn to tell _me_ what to draw.

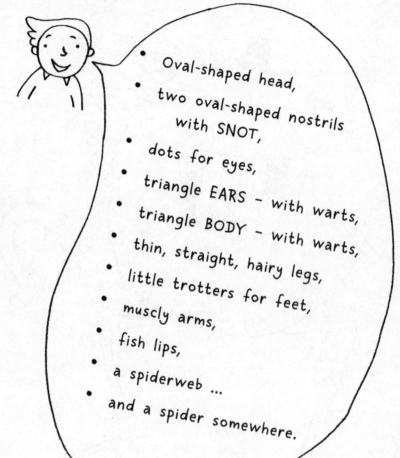

- Oval-shaped head,
- two oval-shaped nostrils with SNOT,
- dots for eyes,
- triangle EARS - with warts,
- triangle BODY - with warts,
- thin, straight, hairy legs,
- little trotters for feet,
- muscly arms,
- fish lips,
- a spiderweb ...
- and a spider somewhere.

I do my best.

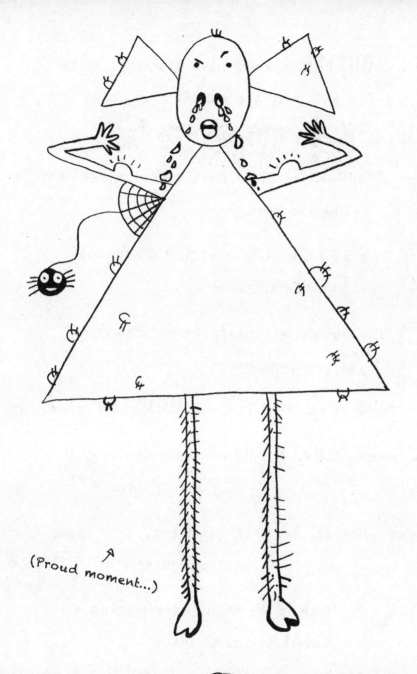

(Proud moment...)

Our **MONSTER** doodles have attracted quite

a few kids who are watching us draw.

"Are you allowed to draw on the ground like that?"

one kid asks.

"It's only **CHALK –** it'll come off,"

I tell them.

"The doodle will disappear when it rains,"

Derek explains.

The kids say they like our **MONSTER** game.

"I'm bringing **CHALK** with me tomorrow,"

one girl says.

"We're going to play that game too,"

another kid tells us.

 "I think we might have started a

CHALK craze," I say.

Before going back to class, we play one more DIFFERENT game. It takes a while but it's worth it.

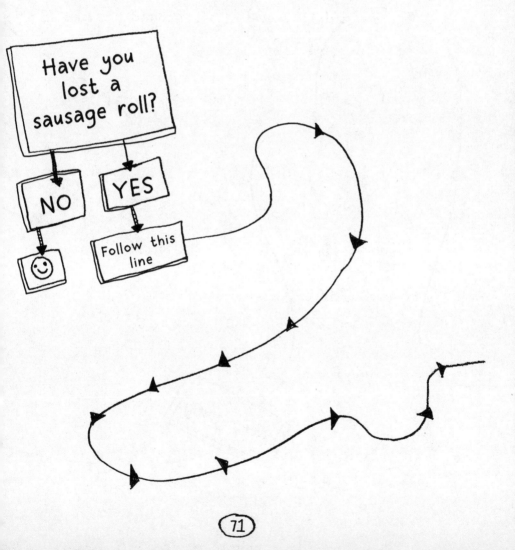

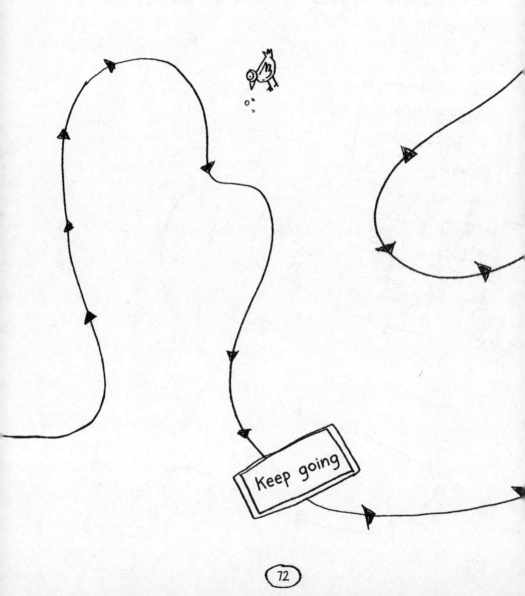

Keep going

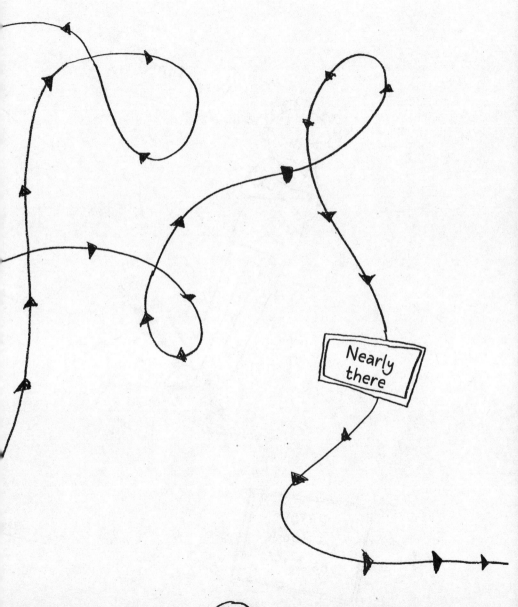

Nearly there

(I think I'm going to need even
more **CHALK** tomorrow.)

CHALK
smiley

In the afternoon, Mr Fullerman tells us we will be making PROPS for the new school play, which is good news for me – I love making stuff.

In case you didn't see the poster, we're putting on **JACK** and **the BEANSTALK,** and Mrs Nap would love us to make some leaves and beans for the beanstalk.  We've got lots of craft materials to use.

Amy puts up her hand to ask a question.

"Sir, do you know our teacher's name yet?" she asks.

(I'd almost forgotten about the supply teacher.)

"Yes I do, Amy. I met her at lunchtime. It's a shame she wasn't able to pop in to meet you all. Her name is..."

"Hello, everyone!"

Mr Fullerman is interrupted by Mrs Mumble making an announcement.

"Mrs Nap has asked me to remind you NOT to write on the audition poster. The auditions are open to → ALL AGES, and not SMALL CABBAGES like it says now. Thank you."

Buster Jones,

I whisper to AMY, as it sounds like something he'd do.

AMY puts up her hand again and says, "Mr Fullerman, you were going to tell us our teacher's name."

I'm really hoping he's not going to say Miss Gravel (fingers crossed).

Yes, her name is...

MISS GRAVEL!

 Sigh ... that's not what I wanted to hear.

There's a general AAAAAWWWWW noise as

the news sinks in around the classroom.

 **"No need for that, Class 5F. Now,**
let's get busy MAKING PROPS!"

Mr Fullerman tells us and shows us how to make

the leaves for the beanstalk and the painted beans.

Draw the shape here.

Pipe cleaners

Attach the leaf

PAINT

I'm enjoying the lesson, but it's still not helping the

Miss Gravel situation.

We're in FULL beanstalk-making mode when there's a **KNOCK** at the door. It's Caretaker Stan.

"Sorry to disturb you, Mr Fullerman, but there's a problem in the stock room," Stan says.

"What's happened?"

"Well, I noticed the door was open, and as you know it's always supposed to be locked," Stan says.

The WHOLE class are listening now as kids aren't allowed in the stock room on their own. It's where all the exciting stuff is kept. I notice there's *glitter* falling off Caretaker Stan's arm as he talks.

"I went inside to see who was in there and the MESS I found! Things knocked over, glitter everywhere, and don't get me started on the BUBBLE WRAP!"

"I definitely locked the door, Stan," Mr Fullerman tells him.

"LOOK at this poster card — it looks like it's been CHEWED!" Caretaker Stan holds up the card.

As soon as he says the word "CHEWED", Marcus and I look at each other and then I say DRAMATICALLY, "Did you HEAR THAT? Maybe Mark Clump was right about it being a **CREATURE**."

"Really? More like **Buster Jones** has been in there messing stuff up. That's the sort of thing he'd do," **AMY** suggests.

Then something happens that I'm really NOT EXPECTING at ALL.

Marcus only goes and AGREES WITH ME!
"I think Tom's right. There is something going
on. The card's been chewed in the stock room and
my sausage roll's been eaten!"

 "Don't forget the cardboard box ," I add.

"That was definitely the *WIND,* Tom,"
AMY says.

"Actually, I think it was the *WIND* too,"
Marcus adds.
  (Marcus agreeing with me didn't last long.)

Mr Fullerman tells Caretaker Stan that he'll
try and find out what happened.

"Do you know anything, Class 5F?"
Mr Fullerman asks us. We don't – not YET anyway.

We carry on making beanstalks for the play while discussing **WHAT** could be causing the problems around school (apart from **Buster**).

Wasn't me.

The beanstalks are coming along nicely – they look better than I thought they would. Even if the play's a bit rubbish, the beanstalks will look great.

Snake

When the bell goes for home time,
Mr Fullerman says...

"See you all in a WEEK.
Be good, and try not to scrape your
chairs on the way out..."

SSSSSCCRRAAAAPPPPE

"Oh, my..."

(Normally Mr Fullerman would call
us back, but he doesn't today.)

(83)

I meet Derek in the corridor when Marcus walks
past me and says,

"So, Tom, are you still up for helping me
with my food trap tomorrow?"

"Sure!" I say and Derek LOOKS at me
in a 'what's going on?' kind of way.

"I said I'd help him find the sausage roll
thief," I try and explain.
"Good luck with that. There's a lot of kids
in this school – it could be anyone!"
Derek says.

"Or any THING..."
I agree.
"Imagine what the newspaper headlines would be!"
Derek adds.

"Mystery monster steals lunch!" I laugh.

Derek and I make up more headlines as we walk home.

But it's the REAL one outside the shop that gets our attention...

"Hey, Derek!
A MUSIC FESTIVAL
in OAKFIELD TOWN!"
I shout.
We're both officially
EXCITED. ☆

"Shall we go in for a QUICK read?" I suggest.

"It's all in <u>tomorrow's</u> paper. We can find out who's playing then – IF the shopkeeper lets us,"

Derek says.

"Or we could buy our OWN copy?" I suggest, which is an excellent idea (we just need some money).

As we're chatting about the MUSIC festival, I look up, and at the end of the street I SPOT something walking round the corner that looks a lot like BANDIT!

I GRAB Derek's arm and make him run with me to try and catch up.

"What's up?" Derek asks.

"BANDIT ALERT!" I shout.

We keep RUNNING to the end of the street, but **BANDIT** has disappeared and we don't know which way he went.

"Awwww, we missed him!" I say.

"He must live around here somewhere. I'm sure we'll see **BANDIT** again soon," Derek says, which is true, but it's still annoying we didn't get to see him.

I ask Derek, "Can I come with you the next time you take Rooster for a walk?"

"Of course! It's more fun with both of us," Derek tells me.

Sometimes I pretend that Rooster is my dog.

If he <u>was</u> my dog, I'd
train him to **CHEW** Delia's
stuff and not mine.

Unless it was my homework - that would be
a useful excuse if I hadn't finished it.
I've used Rooster as an excuse before, but
Mr Fullerman doesn't always believe me.

Evidence

"Sorry, sir, Rooster ate my homework."

AGAIN?

Derek and I arrange to meet up early tomorrow
morning. I even set my alarm so I won't be LATE.

(OAKCHELLA, here we come!)

 Morning! →

I forgot how LOUD the alarm on my digital watch is, but at least I'm awake now.  BEEP! BEEP! BEEP!

We don't get the local paper that often, unless one of the family is actually in it.

SPOONTASTIC!

Bob Gates did a sponsored spoon-playing to raise money for the Leafy Green Old Folks' Home.

So it's a SURPRISE to see Delia is up before me and READING a copy at the breakfast table.

She must have got up really early to get it. This is handy for me, as now I don't have to buy one. I can read HERS instead.

(Also, I don't have any money.)

"Hey, Delia - is that today's local paper?" I ask her.

"It might be," she mumbles.

"Is there anything in there about the
OAKCHELLA MUSIC FESTIVAL?"

 "Why do you want to know?"

"Because I want to find out who's playing and how to get **TICKETS**," I tell her, HOPING she'll let me see it.

"I'm reading it. Go and have your breakfast, Tom," Delia tells me.

"Can't you just tell me who's playing?" I say again.

"Leave me alone - I'm trying to read in peace!" Delia mutters, then covers the paper so I can't see it, which is annoying.

"Can I read it AFTER you, then?" I ask her.

"Sorry, Tom, I'm taking it with me," she tells me, then turns the page over.

I manage to get a quick GLIMPSE of something that says, **FREE TICKETS FOR THE FESTIVAL,** which is interesting.

I'm about to ask her a question  when Mum and Dad walk in. They're surprised to see Delia reading the local paper too.

Whoa...

"What's the news then, Delia?" Dad asks.

"You're not in it, are you? Do we have to buy copies for the grandparents?" Mum wants to know, then adds...

"Only if you're in there for GOOD reasons, of course."

"I'm NOT in the paper!" Delia tells them grumpily.

"Oakfield Town is having a music festival. It's in the paper, but Delia won't let me see it," I tell Mum and Dad.

"That's because it's MY PAPER," she says, getting annoyed.

"Is that OAKCHELLA? I've seen posters in town about it," Dad says.

"Can we go? PLEEEEEEASE? I've never been to a festival before." I do my best pleading voice as I really want to go.

"It's too expensive, Tom, and we can't really afford FOUR **TICKETS.** Especially after paying to fix the shed roof," Mum tells me.

"It's not like I didn't TRY and do it myself, Rita.
I think the FESTIVAL would be fun, don't you?"
Dad says.

"Not really, and I definitely wouldn't be up

    for camping either," Mum tells him.

   (Dad seems KEEN - Mum not so much.

    I'm going to keep asking them anyway.)

"Hey, Delia, show Mum and Dad the **FREE TICKETS**
page - we could enter that!" I suggest while
LEANING over to give her a hand.

EXCUSE ME,
TOM... Do you MIND?

     Delia closes the paper up.

   "I don't need **FREE TICKETS** because

   Avril's already bought ours. We're going to

the FESTIVAL with our friends."

Mum and Dad look almost as SURPRISED as I do. "That's not FAIR! If Delia's going, why can't we?" I say.

They spend the next five minutes asking Delia questions about who she's going with, which gives me a chance to have another sneaky GLANCE at the FESTIVAL stuff.

"LOOK! It says here we can enter our names to get the **FREE TICKETS,"** I tell Mum and Dad again.

"I suppose it's worth a try," Dad agrees.

"We'll see," Mum says, which usually means NO.

Delia is fed up with me reading her paper and takes it with her as she leaves.

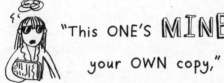

"This ONE'S MINE. You'll have to get your OWN copy," she says.

So I try one more time in my best pleading voice.

"PLEEASSSSEEE can we go?"

"I'll see if I can get another paper," Dad tells me, which makes me more hopeful until

Mum adds...

"FESTIVALS and me just don't seem to MIX, I'm afraid."

"That's not what I remember!"

Dad LAUGHs.

"Is it that time already? Come on, Tom, hurry up or you'll be late for school," Mum says quickly, then reminds me to take my packed lunch as I go off to meet Derek.

The first thing we do (apart from high-five) is go to the shop and look at the sign outside.

It's all about the OAKCHELLA FESTIVAL.

There's a whole five minutes to spare before school starts, which is PLENTY of time to go inside and have a quick read.

"We can find out who's playing," Derek says.

"Morning, BOYS. Can I help you to BUY anything?" the shopkeeper asks.

"We're just deciding what to get..." Derek tells her, as we don't have any money. Then we stand in front of the paper and try to read as much as possible.

When she's not looking, Derek does a quick **FLICK** through, hoping she won't notice.

(She does.)

"It would be SO much easier if you boys just BOUGHT a paper," she tells us.

We pretend to be looking for money when she SIGHS and says "BE QUICK!" then lets us have a better look. RESULT!

98

I can't see ANY bands I recognize yet.
No 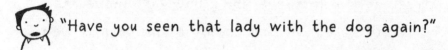, which is a BIG shame.
While we're having a quick read I ask her a question.

 "Have you seen that lady with the dog again?"

"She was in this morning, I think,"

the shopkeeper tells us.

"WITH BANDIT?" I say enthusiastically, and
we put the paper back as this is FAR more interesting.

"No dog today that I noticed. You boys
need to get going or you'll be late."

Which is true as we have ONE MINUTE to spare.

"Thanks for the read!" I say as we **RUN** out
of the shop and only just make it
to school. We avoid Mr Keen by
going to the dinner hall door.

Only this time ... it's **LOCKED.**

Huh?

I **RATTLE** the door handle and give it a PULL, but we still can't get inside and we're forced to go back to the main door.

Mr Keen is there LOOKING for latecomers.

"Hello, you two. Hurry up. Better not be late again this week," he says.

"Sorry, sir. It was REALLY BUSY out there and we got slowed down," I explain. It's a RUBBISH excuse but it's all I can think of under pressure.

"You don't want to make a BAD impression on your NEW teacher, do you, Tom?"

 "No, sir," I say. I'd completely
forgotten about the supply teacher.

We head to class and Derek wishes me luck.
"Hope Miss Grrrravelll isn't too ...

GRRIMMmmmmm,"

he says to make me laugh.

I'm trying to THINK of a better excuse in
case she asks me why I'm late.
Being a NEW teacher, Miss Gravel won't have
heard ANY of these excuses from me, which is handy.

TOP OF MY LIST:

• My sister Delia wouldn't get out of the bathroom.

• A vicious dog cornered me. I had to hide.

• I stopped to help an old lady across the road.

• I hurt my foot and was forced to
LIMP all the way to school.

I'm still thinking of excuses when I walk into class and hear a voice say...

> # Hello, Tom,
> ## nice to see you again!
> ## Take a seat, and please EXPLAIN
> ## to us all why you're LATE.

"Huh ... errrrrrr?"

Everyone is SILENT and waiting to hear my

EXCUSE.

But I can't speak because I've just realized who our supply teacher is...

IT'S THE LADY FROM THE SHOP WITH **BANDIT!**

SHE'S MISS GRAVEL!

"Did you stop off at the shop AGAIN, Tom?" she asks.

"No ... I ... I..." I start to say, but the pressure gets to me and I BLURT out the wrong excuse. "I twisted my ankle and had to LIMP all the way to school. I've been in PAIN..." I grimace for effect.

"Oh dear, I'm very sorry to hear that. Please hurry up and take a seat," Miss Gravel says in a FIERCE way.

"My foot's still SORE," I tell her and shuffle to my desk slowly then sit down CAREFULLY.

"Do you need to see the school nurse, or for us to call your parents?" Miss Gravel wants to know.

"I'll be fine – I think," I say as I don't want Mum and Dad to know anything. Now I know WHY Miss Gravel was asking SO many questions about our school in the shop.

No wonder the secret door was locked!

Why did I have to go and tell her all about it?

(I am a twit.)

AMY looks down at my leg.

"Do you already know Miss Gravel then?"

"Not really. We just saw her in the shop.
She has a very cool dog," I say.

"Which foot did you hurt?" AMY asks.

"Errrrr ... this one?" I say, holding up my
RIGHT foot.

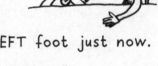

"You were limping on your LEFT foot just now.
Stick to the same one at least."

"Good thinking," I tell her before
Miss Gravel says...

"ABSOLUTELY NO TALKING IN CLASS."

(She's looking at us.)

"What's your name, please?" Miss Gravel asks.

"AMY PORTER."

"I'll remember that. And WE'VE already met, haven't we, Tom?"

 "Yes, Miss Grovel."

As soon as I say the wrong name, I try and correct myself, but everyone heard. A few kids laugh, but not for long.

 "I mean Miss Gravel - Miss Gravel."

(Too late.) Hmmmm...

She GLARES at me, then stands in front of the class and says, really slowly (and slightly spookily), "My name is Miss Gravel. I'll write it on the board in case you get confused. Shall we all say it together?"

"MISS GRAVEL."

The class repeats her name. No one will get it wrong now, including me.

"Let's get on with the register, shall we? We're going to have such a FANTASTIC time over the next few days, I can tell!"

(I'm not so sure about that.)

Marcus writes something down on a bit of paper and passes it to me under the table, which is **RISKY.**

I open it up and read it like I'm casually looking down at my hand.

SHE'S STRICT!
COME BACK,
MR FULLERMAN!

PS – sausage roll plan
in action at lunchtime.

(I'd forgotten about the sausage roll...)

The **WHOLE** of our lesson with Miss Gravel is in complete

S
I
L
E
N
C
E

↓

Which is unusual for our class, but Miss Gravel doesn't want anyone talking or making ANY noise at all. Leroy Lewis keeps **COUGHING** and she gives him some water. Brad Galloway sniffs a few times and she hands him a tissue. Miss Gravel gets even 'more annoyed by chairs **SCRAPING** than Mr Fullerman did.

Sniff
Sniff

"NO **SCRAPING** CHAIRS, 5F!"

Miss **G**ravel tells us sternly. We all keep so quiet
we can hear **M**r **S**procket's class next door,
who sound like they're having a really **FUN**
time and **LAUGHING** a **lot**.

Ha!
Ha!
Ha!

It's like sitting next to someone who's eating
a sandwich that's MUCH nicer than yours.

Talking of food...

Marcus is DESPERATE to tell me about his sausage roll TRAP, so as soon as Miss Gravel says,

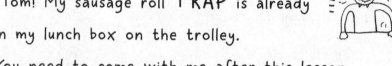 "You may talk QUIETLY now." He's OFF.

"Tom! My sausage roll TRAP is already in my lunch box on the trolley.
You need to come with me after this lesson STRAIGHT AWAY!"

"Sure, OK," I say, but I'd much rather just go and eat my own lunch. (I don't say that, though.)
When the bell goes, Miss Gravel stops everyone from charging off and says...

"NO SCRAPING chairs. Leave quietly and no running either." Then she asks me how my BAD FOOT is. (I'd forgotten about that!)

"Still very sore, Miss Gravel," I say, then I remember to LIMP as I walk out of class.

I keep LIMPING all the way out of the classroom and down to where the lunch trolleys are. (It takes a while.)

Marcus is already there and peering out from behind a wall.

"You took your time," he says.

"I've got a BAD FOOT, remember?"

"Oh yeah - anyway, the trap is inside my lunch box. Anyone who takes it will not want to eat it, THAT'S for sure," he tells me.

"Sounds like something Granny Mavis would make," I laugh. Marcus doesn't get my joke.

Glum →  "Is it a FAKE sausage roll, then?"

"No, but **NO ONE** will want to eat it. You'll see why. I need to keep **WATCH** – that's why I'm hiding. You should as well, that way if anyone goes near my lunch box, we can CATCH THEM!" Marcus tells me.

"You could put a BIG fake spider on your lunch box. That would scare them away too," I suggest.

"That's not a bad idea," Marcus says as more and more kids come down to lunch.

I'm getting hungry and I want to go and eat. Everyone is collecting their food from the trolleys so for a while we can't see it. I'm not really paying attention when Marcus starts shouting...

My lunch box!

It's GONE!
Someone's taken my
FOOD again!

OPEN

 arcus runs over to his open lunch box.

"How did that happen? We were keeping WATCH!"

he shouts.

"Kind of..." I point out, as we were chatting

quite a lot.

 "Someone's TAKEN my sausage roll!

My trap didn't work," Marcus sighs.

We look around to see if there are ANY

SUSPECTS here or in the dinner hall, but it's

just the usual group of kids. I pick up my

lunch box as I don't want to lose THAT as well.

"They only took my sausage roll, not

my sandwich," he tells me, holding up a really

disgusting plastic bag.

(114)

"YUCK! It's all mouldy. No wonder they left it," I say.

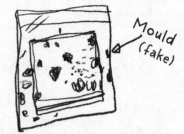
Mould (fake)

"It's not REAL mould. It's printed on the inside of the BAG. I put my sausage roll in one as well to try and PUT OFF the thief! I'm going to tell a teacher – I'm not happy about this," Marcus complains and **STOMPS** off to the teachers' table.

At least I can go and EAT now. I'm really hungry. I find Derek and tell him everything that's happened. When Marcus comes and joins us, he's still **CROSS.**

"The teachers are going to keep a lookout for the sausage roll thief," he says, then takes out his sandwich again.

"EEEEEEeeeeeWWWWWwww!"

Everyone round the table thinks the sandwich looks
DISGUSTING.

AMY looks up and says, "That's GROSS,
Marcus. It's all mouldy! You can't eat that!"

"It's just on the BAG - it's FAKE!
But whoever took my sausage roll didn't
care it was mouldy, so my plan didn't exactly
work out."

Marcus holds the bag up so we can all see it. Then
he takes out his sandwich and eats it.

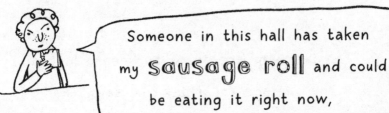

Someone in this hall has taken
my sausage roll and could
be eating it right now,

Marcus says dramatically.

He could be right.

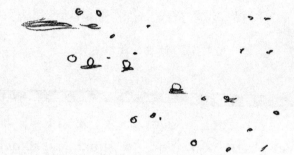

I'm going to try and get some of the FAKE
mouldy bags to use at home. They'll be excellent for
stopping Delia (or my cousins) from pinching
my NICE BISCUITS.

A fake spider might do the trick too
(maybe I can use them
BOTH together).

We've taken SO long to finish our lunch (mostly
due to chat about sausage rolls and mouldy food)
that the little kids have NABBED the Champ square.

Its OK though as Derek's brought his chalk
with him, so I suggest we could go and
play WHAT MONSTER? again.

"No, thanks – I've got more important things to do, like look for sausage roll SUSPECTS," arcus says.

Which is fair enough.

"How do you play **WHAT MONSTER?**" **AMY** asks.

"It's EASY! We can show you the **MONSTERS** we made yesterday," I say.

"If they're still there," **D** erek points out.

We all head over to where we drew them and **AMY** says,

> Is that part of the game too?

SOMEONE has added a
GREAT BIG SPEECH BUBBLE that says:

(Proud moment...)

"No, it's NOT!" I tell AMY.

"It's quite FUNNY though,"
Solid laughs.

We're so busy looking at the MONSTER that we don't notice Miss Gravel is on playground duty with Mrs Worthington AND they're walking towards us.

"QUICK! Don't let Miss Gravel see THAT!" Derek says.

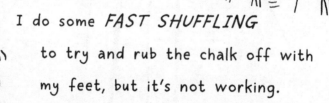

I do some FAST SHUFFLING to try and rub the chalk off with my feet, but it's not working.

"WHAT ARE WE GOING TO DO?" Norman yells, jumping up and down.

"Don't panic!" I tell him.

Then I **lie** on the ground to cover the speech
bubble up JUST IN TIME.

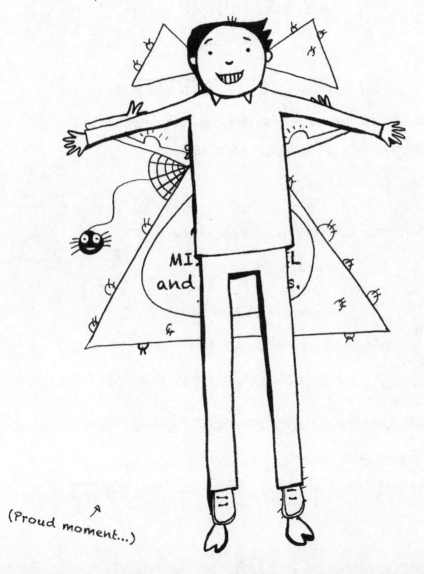

(Proud moment...)

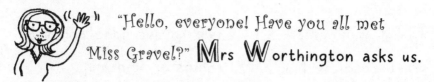

"Hello, everyone! Have you all met Miss Gravel?" Mrs Worthington asks us.

Everyone says "YES", including me from the ground. Miss Gravel looks down.

"I've met most of you. Is this where you hang out at lunchtime then?"

she wants to know.

"I'm having a REST, Miss Gravel. I'm tired and my foot's still sore,"

I try and explain, but

it's all a bit awkward.

Then Derek helps me out.

"We're playing a game too, aren't we?"

"Yes, we are," says AMY.

"Are we?" Norman wonders.

"That sounds interesting. Don't let us stop you. I'd LOVE to see what game it is," Miss Gravel says.

(She's not the only one.)

Derek gives a piece of chalk to everyone and they start to draw **EXTRA** things around me.

"See, Miss Gravel, we're making
Tom look like a **FUNNY MONSTER**,"

Derek explains.

"I can see that!" Miss Gravel says.

"Mind you don't draw on Tom's clothes!"
Mrs Worthington tells them.

"Good point," I agree.

"As long as Tom stays still he'll be FINE!"
Florence says. I'm trying not to move as I don't want
Miss Gravel to see the speech bubble.

"See you in class, and Tom, I hope your foot feels

better after the rest."

 "I hope so too," I say and we all BREATHE
a sigh of relief as they walk away.

Before I get up, everyone admires their drawings.

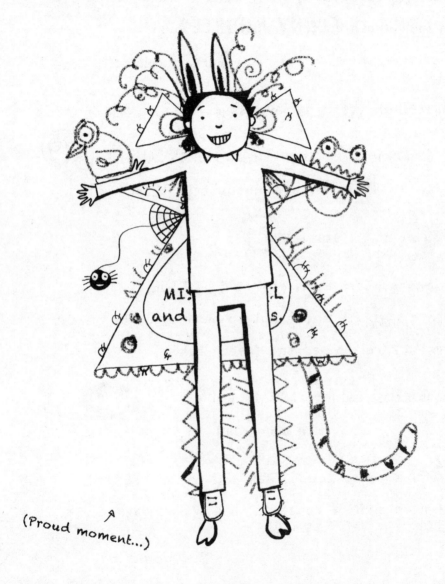

(Proud moment...)

"You can move now, Tom," **AMY** says then gets her water bottle and pours it over the speech bubble, which disappears.

"Why didn't you do that earlier?" I ask her.

"I just thought of it. Besides, I liked that game. BUNNY EARS really suit you!"

AMY LAUGHs.

"So do spiky legs," Florence adds.

"Well it's someone else's turn to get DRAWN around next time!" I let everyone know.

"I'll do it! If we can FIND some space to draw," **N**orman says then points out that all the kids around us are DRAWING with **CHALK.**

"It's a **WHAT MONSTER?** chalk CRAZE!" **D**erek says. True...

(Even the CHAMP kids have started doing it.)

Seems like everyone is copying our doodles.

Hopscotch →

8   9

7

5   6

4

2   3

1

Walking back to class, **AMY** reminds me to **LIMP** with the LEFT foot. "Just in case **M**iss **G**ravel sees you," she says.

Then Marcus tells me I've got a **CHALK FACE** on my back.

It looks weird.

"Thanks for letting me know."

Norman BRUSHES it off, which is nice of him.

"Why did you have a **CHALK FACE** on your back?" Marcus asks.

"It's a L O N G story," I start to say when he interrupts.

"Aren't you going to ask me how I got on?"

"OK, how did you get on?" I ask.

"NOT VERY WELL – although I did find a LOT of food crumbs behind a TREE," he says. Which could be something, who knows?

Miss Gravel is about to take the afternoon
register when a really strange wailing
noise starts from OUTSIDE.

OOOOOOOOOWWWWwwww

Before anyone can STAND UP to take a LOOK,
Miss Gravel says...

 **"SIT DOWN! Nobody move."**

(Gulp.)

Julia Morton puts up her hand.
"Please, miss, what's that scary noise?"
she wants to know. (We ALL DO!)

"It's a **WEREWOLF...**" someone GASPS.

"Or a **MONSTER!**" someone else SHOUTS.

Miss Gravel has had ENOUGH and begins to say,
"There is NOTHING to..."

...When it happens AGAIN!

OOOOOoooooWWWWwwww!

THIS TIME even Miss Gravel looks SURPRISED.
She walks to the window and takes
a L O N G look outside. I can hear her
muttering, It can't be?

Mark Clump is busy telling everyone around him
that it sounds like a BIG CAT or a BEAR, Don't
mind me.
Grrrrrr which isn't helping much.
Grrrrrr

The noise starts to get a bit softer
but everyone in class OOOOOoooooWWWWwwww!
is still imagining WHAT it MIGHT be.
(And not in a good way.)
Miss Gravel turns around slowly and
STARES at us.

"OK, where were we? I have something Mr Fullerman left for you to do. He said it's your FAVOURITE subject..."

Julia Morton puts her hand up once more. "But, Miss Gravel – WHAT was that noise?" she asks.

"It was NOTHING for you to worry about, and it's GONE now so the only thing you have to concern yourself with is ..."

"My missing SAUSAGE ROLL!" Marcus blurts out, which gets a stare from Miss Gravel.

"No, Marcus, the spelling test... AND the school play AUDITIONS. Let's not forget about that too."

Miss Gravel manages to expertly change the subject and makes us all get back to work.

While we're doing the spelling test,
Miss Gravel keeps a KEEN EYE on everyone
so it's impossible to take ANY sneaky
peeks 👀 👀 at AMY's work
(which might have helped me).

I can still hear a very faint

OOOOooooooWWWWwwww!

noise in the distance that no one else seems
that bothered about now.

Especially Marcus, who is already planning ANOTHER
trap to catch the sausage roll thief, so I make a
suggestion.

"Why don't you just bring something
BAD to eat, like ... a broccoli BUN.

No one would steal THAT!"

"Because I like sausage rolls. What's a broccoli bun
anyway?"

"EEErrrrrr... it's 🥦 broccoli ... 🍔 in a bun.
Granny Mavis makes them," I explain.

"You're right – that does sound BAD," Marcus says.

 Miss Gravel tells us she'll give us our
test results tomorrow.

"We will be doing the play auditions too. ANYONE who wants to take
part should go to the HALL at lunchtime," she reminds us.

"I'll be there," Marcus says confidently.

Looking over his shoulder I can SEE the idea he's
been working on to catch the thief.

I'm not sure it'll work though...

(Ambitious...)

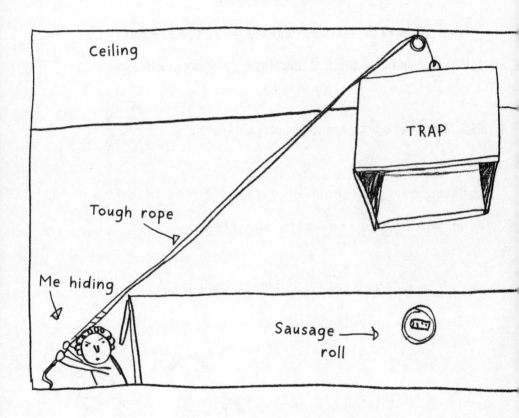

Tomorrow will be interesting, I can tell.

When the bell goes for home time, Miss Gravel asks us to STAND and push our chairs in silently and we do.

(Mr Fullerman would be impressed.)
I even remember to LIMP "⌐⌐" out of the classroom to meet Derek, who's in a really good mood. ☺

"I've had the best time in the hall practising "⌐⌐" for the play auditions. What did you do this afternoon, Tom?" he asks me.

"Spelling test," I say gloomily.
"Did you hear that WEIRD wailing noise?"
I ask him to see what he thinks it might have been.

"I didn't hear anything," he says.

"Yeah. It was probably nothing..." I sigh.

Or maybe it wasn't?

OAKFIELD GAZETTE

BIG CAT GOES MISSING!

There's even more on the other side ... about the MUSIC FESTIVAL and who's won the FIRST pair of tickets.

OAKFIELD GAZETTE

OAKCHELLA! FIRST TICKETS WON BY VERA (86 Years Young)

ENTER EVERY DAY this WEEK to WIN!

"Vera lives at the LEAFY GREEN OLD FOLKS' HOME, I think."

"If Vera is going, we HAVE to go too," he says.

I agree.

We take a quick look in the shop to find out more...

The shopkeeper has **BAD** NEWS for us.
"Sorry, boys, ALL the papers have sold
out. It's the FREE festival tickets, I think –
they've been VERY popular. You can BUY a
copy tomorrow though," she points out.

"We will..." Derek says. (We probably won't.)

I'm still **LIMPING** as we walk home
when Derek tells me I don't have
to any more.
"Oh, yeah... I knew that," I say.
Before Derek goes into his house I remind him
about the play auditions.

We high-five and I head inside – STRAIGHT
into the kitchen to **LOOK** for **SNACKS.**

SNACKS!

I can't find ANY snacks BUT on the table there's a COPY of the latest local PAPER.

Which is BRILLIANT!

"FREE TICKETS, here I come!" I say to myself and try and find the right page.

"Is THAT my paper you've taken?" Delia says when she sees me.

"No - Mum or Dad must have bought it, so it's almost MINE." I put Delia straight. I can tell she wants to READ it, so I start looking at every page really slowly.

I find the story on the missing BIG CAT, which isn't EXACTLY what I was expecting.

(Like a TIGER or something WILD.)

BIG CAT FOUND IN TREE!

When Dad comes in from his shed he's IMPRESSED I'm reading. "I'll have to buy papers more often."

"I'm looking for the **FREE** FESTIVAL **tickets** page," I tell Dad.

"No way! I really don't want my parents or little brother spoiling my fun," Delia grumbles.

"**N**o one wants to spoil your FUN, Delia,"
Dad tells her.

"I might – IF I was there," I mutter.

 "Good job you're not going then, isn't it?"
Delia says, rubbing it in.

Mum comes back from work and **FLOPS**
down into a chair.

"I'm EXHAUSTED. Are you all still talking
about the FESTIVAL? Did you SEE the
local paper – Vera from LEAFY GREEN WON
TWO tickets!" Mum laughs.

"Vera's about a hundred and fifty – why does
she want to go?" Delia says.

"To have some FUN just like you!" Dad tells her.

"**SEE?** EVERYONE'S going apart from us!"

I decided to remind them AGAIN, hoping it might change their minds.

"There'll be other FESTIVALS, Tom — I promise. We couldn't go now anyway. I've just told the Jacksons from work we're free that weekend to come over and stay," Mum says.

"Have you? Oh... Tom won't want to come with us to a WORK DO," Dad says.

He's RIGHT, I don't.

"I'll go with Vera to the FESTIVAL!" I suggest, which is a good idea.

"I thought you could stay with your cousins. Uncle Kevin and Aunty Alice said it was fine."

"I'd rather go to the FESTIVAL. Hey, Delia — I can come with you!"

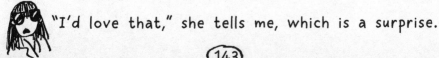

"I'd love that," she tells me, which is a surprise.

143

"REALLY?"

I say, thinking she actually might MEAN it.

"I'm joking, Tom. Of course I'm not going with you. I'm going with **Avril** and my friends," she adds.

"Oh, that reminds me – your grandparents will pop in to make sure you're OK while we're gone," Mum lets Delia know in case she has any **PARTY** PLANS.

(That's happened before.)

"Right – I'm glad that's all sorted. How's everyone's DAY been?" Mum wants to know.

"Good, thanks," Dad says cheerily while Delia just shrugs her shoulders. I close up the paper so I can concentrate on telling everyone about **M**iss **G**ravel and Marcus's sausage roll disappearing.

Straight away Delia asks me if she can have the paper now.

"I'm still reading it!" I tell her even though I'm not. "I want to find the **FREE FESTIVAL TICKET** page just in case. It might be our ONLY chance to go," I say HOPEFULLY.

"Actually, Tom, the page isn't THERE because I've already filled it in and ENTERED the **FREE TICKET** draw," Dad says, which I'm very HAPPY about. :)

"I hope we WIN!" I shout.

"Thousands of people have entered – you've got NO chance of winning them," Delia grumbles.

"You're probably RIGHT, and we can't go now anyway," Mum says.

"I could still go though," I point out.

"Paper, please," Delia asks and I reluctantly hand it over.

"Come on, Tom – tell us about your day at school," Mum says. She's trying to stop me from thinking about the FESTIVAL, I can tell.

"Miss Gravel the supply teacher is the STRICTEST teacher EVER in the WHOLE WIDE WORLD. We've got her for the rest of the week too," I groan.

"She sounds like MY kind of teacher," Mum says and smiles, which is a bit annoying.

"ALSO, Marcus has had quite a few sausage rolls TAKEN from his lunchbox."

"Who took them?" Dad asks.

It's a **MYSTERY.** It could be a kid in school, OR Mark Clump thinks it might be some kind of creature. There's been a **LOT** of ODD things going on in school.

"What kind of things?" Mum wants to know.

So I tell them about *MOVING* boxes, food being pinched and LOUD WAILING sounds that even **M**iss **G**ravel couldn't explain.

"Sounds like a NORMAL school day to me," Dad **LAUGHS.**

"AND the auditions for the school play are on tomorrow," I remember to tell them.

"That's come round FAST. What is it this time?" Mum asks.

"JACK AND THE BEANSTALK," I say.

"Excellent! Can we help out in any way?"

"Two **TICKETS** to the FESTIVAL would be GOOD,"
 I suggest.

"Nice try, Tom," Mum and Dad both say.

"I'm the ONLY person NOT going to OAKCHELLA,"
I tell them.

"I'm sure Derek's not going."
Mum is trying to make me feel better.

"No, I don't think he is," I mumble.

"Well, you're not the only person NOT going then,
are you?" Dad points out.

(148)

"esides, I'm sure you'll have a FANTASTIC
time with the cousins. ncle evin told me
he's got something *AMAZING* planned
for you all to do."

 "It'll be GREAT!" Mum says enthusiastically.

"You'll have more fun than we will at your
mother's WORK party!" Dad tells me and Mum
gives him a LŎŎK.
(I'm not so sure - we could be going birdwatching again.)

'm getting ready for bed later on when erek
starts tapping at his window, so I go and
see what he wants.

 He's holding up a sign that says...

I'm going to OAKCHELLA! YES!

I write a sign back that says...

YEAH! Lucky you!

and TRY to be pleased for him, but it's not easy. 😕

School Play Audition Day

The next day as we're walking to school, Derek is trying VERY hard **NOT** to talk about the FESTIVAL as he knows I don't have a **TICKET.**

Which is nice of him, but I keep asking him questions anyway, like...

"How many **TICKETS** have you got then?"

"One for me and two for my parents. We'd have got one for you if I'd known. Maybe we still could?"

"THAT would be AMAZING. But I'm supposed to be staying at my cousins' doing something 'SPECIAL'. I bet it won't be though."

I'm feeling a bit more POSITIVE about my chances of going to **OAKCHELLA**, right until we walk past the latest **NEWSPAPER HEADLINE** outside the shop.

OAKFIELD GAZETTE

OAKCHELLA FESTIVAL TICKETS SOLD OUT

BIG SUCCESS!

"You might still WIN the **FREE TICKETS** though?" Derek suggests.

"Maybe..." I sigh.

I try and think about the PLAY auditions instead.

"It should be FUN, as long as Miss Gravel isn't in CHARGE!" I tell Derek.

Morning, Class 5F.
I'll be doing the play
auditions with
you today...

(I spoke too soon.)

Miss Gravel asks me how my FOOT is and for
some reason I start LIMPING again.

"It's still a bit SORE, actually," I tell her and
gently sit at my desk. I don't know WHY I
said that.

AMY and Marcus are already sitting down
and I notice Marcus is holding on to his
bag VERY tightly.

AMY nudges me and says,

"Is it my imagination or can you smell FOOD
around here?"

I sniff the air a few times.

"I know what you mean. It smells like ...
sniff ... sausage roll?"

SNIFF
SNIFF

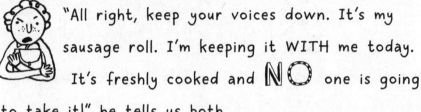 Marcus PULLS his bag tighter towards him.

"All right, keep your voices down. It's my sausage roll. I'm keeping it WITH me today. It's freshly cooked and NO one is going to take it!" he tells us both.

 (It does smell really nice.)

 Miss Gravel begins to do her SLOW handclap thing and starts to EXPLAIN what we'll be doing today.

Everyone listens in SILENCE.

"The school play auditions are in the HALL this morning. IF you don't want to take part, you can go to the LIBRARY... There are plenty of MATHS worksheets to do.

Hands up for that please?"

(Only two go up...)

The show of hands for the play auditions is a lot more popular.

We go to the hall and Marcus is still clutching his bag. Everybody who's there is divided into groups and given a different-coloured STICKER.

I'm in the RED GROUP with some of my class and Derek – which is nice.

Miss Gravel is being quite STRICT and STOPS all the chatter with a FIERCE STARE.

She then tells us all,

"Good luck, everyone, and remember there are plenty of parts to go round. Thank you for coming. Now, I'll hand you over to Mrs Nap."

Mrs Nap calls the RED group up FIRST.

(That's us...)

I feel a bit NERVOUS because everyone in the hall is WATCHING us (including Miss Gravel).
Mrs Nap wants us to warm up and SHAKE ourselves out.

Norman has already started.

Mrs Nap stops to ask Marcus to put his bag down as he's STILL HOLDING it.
Reluctantly, he hides it behind the curtain

on the stage.

"Now, imagine the GIANT is
coming towards you and CHASING everyone.
Where are you going to go? Do you turn and FACE
the GIANT? Put yourself in THAT situation...
I want you to SHOW us what you're feeling..."

(So we do.)

Julia Morton is SCREAMING,

 "SAVE ME from the GIANT!"

Everyone is running in different directions, waving their arms around and bumping into each other. Brad Galloway is just **SHOUTING** as loudly as he can.

I join in yelling things like,

"The GIANT is COMING!

It's GOING TO EAT US!"

Mrs Nap looks a bit alarmed and tries to calm us all down but some kids can't hear over the shouting.

Everyone hears Miss Gravel though...

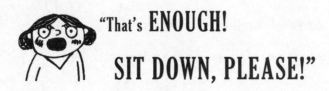 "That's **ENOUGH!**

SIT DOWN, PLEASE!"

"Whoa... Super strict," Derek whispers.

"That's nothing," I say.

Now we're quiet, Mrs Nap takes over again.

"Thank you, Miss Gravel. That was very ENERGETIC acting! Let's do something a little calmer this time. Imagine you're an ANIMAL of some kind and SLOWLY move around the hall as THAT animal," she tells us all. I have a think about what to be and settle on ...

an elephant.

Mostly because it's quite easy to use my arm as a TRUNK.

I walk around trying to work out what everyone else is pretending to be.

I think **AMY'S** a fish of some kind.

Mark Clump's a snake slithering on the floor.

Solid says he's an **OWL** with **OWL EYES.**

Twit-twoo

Brad Galloway is a dog. (Of course he is.)

I have NO idea what Marcus is but he's moving a **LOT.**

Mrs Nap congratulates us all.
"We saw some VERY impressive animals.
Well done, red group. Sit down now please and
let's all watch the BLUE group."

Marcus has taken his bag back again when I
ask him what animal he was pretending to be.

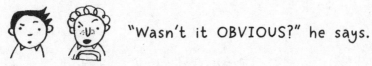

"Wasn't it OBVIOUS?" he says.

"Not really," I tell him.

"I was an OCTOPUS, of course. But I'll make a
much better GIANT if I get the chance," he says.

Mrs Nap is handing out a LIST of the parts
this afternoon so we'll find out then. While the
BLUE group are doing their thing I (stupidly) ask
Marcus if he's going to the FESTIVAL.

"Of course I am - aren't you?" he says.

 "Hopefully," I say as it's better than NO.

I ask a few more of my classmates if they're going and mostly they all say YES.

It feels like nearly the WHOLE of 5F have TICKETS for OAKCHELLA apart from Julia Morton, Paul Jolly and Amber Tully Jones.

Derek keeps trying to stop me from thinking about the FESTIVAL. So at break time he brings out his CHALK ←

Come on, Tom, let's play WHAT MONSTER? again!

If we could find any SPACE we would.

Instead we draw round some other things in the school grounds.

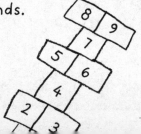

We make some excellent **chalk** BUGS AND
MONSTERS if I do say so myself.

(163)

I find a nice bit of wall and draw a
BIG SNAKE on it before anyone else does...

I give it a sausage roll to eat, which
Derek thinks is funny.
(Marcus might not agree.)

Sausage
ROLL

Marcus is still holding on to his bag when we bump into him heading back to class. "Are you going to the **FESTIVAL, D**erek?" he wants to know.

"Yup, I am," **D**erek says.

"I know YOU'RE probably not, Tom," Marcus adds.

"Thanks for reminding me..."

I **LIMP** back to my seat and Marcus starts talking about his sausage roll again (as if we wanted to know).

"I'm saving it for lunch.

It's SAFELY in my bag this time."

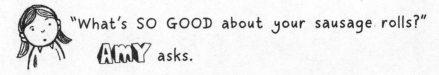

"What's SO GOOD about your sausage rolls?" **AMY** asks.

"When Miss Gravel isn't looking, I'll SHOW you," he tells her.

It's not long before Miss Gravel walks to the back of the classroom, so Marcus gets out his lunch box and hides it behind his bag. "It's the most delicious snack EVER – SEE?" he says, taking the lid off.

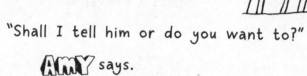

We both peer inside...

"Shall I tell him or do you want to?" AMY says.

"You can..." I sigh because Marcus is NOT going to be happy at all.

"It's GONE! HOW? WHO?
                WHERE ... WHAT?"

"Are you SURE you brought one?" AMY asks him.

"Miss Gravel! Miss Gravel!"

Marcus is shouting for Miss Gravel,

who comes over.

"CALM down, Marcus," she tells him, so he kind

of does.

"Miss Gravel, I had a sausage roll in here

and it's GONE. Someone has stolen it."

"Why are you eating your lunch NOW in class?"

Miss Gravel demands.

"I was just telling AMY and Tom how

delicious it is ... WAS," Marcus tries to

explain.

Then Miss Gravel asks us,

"Do you two know where it went?" like we're suspects.

 "No, Miss Gravel," we both say.

 hen she asks the **WHOLE** CLASS.

Marcus SEEMS to have had a sausage roll go missing. Does ANYONE know anything about it?

No one says a word.

 (Marcus is not very happy.)

For the rest of the lesson he keeps looking at me and **AMY** in a slightly SUSPICIOUS way.

"We didn't take it, Marcus," I tell him again...

So you say,

he replies like he doesn't believe me.

By lunchtime there's a LOT of different rumours FLYING around school about the MISSING sausage roll.

Mark Clump isn't helping by telling MORE WILD animal stories and neither is the SNAKE doodle I drew on the wall. I was only making it UP, but some kids think it's what REALLY happened.

This big!

Whooa!

Oh my...

Marcus is suspicious of EVERYONE now and keeps asking questions like he's a detective.

Where were you at EXACTLY ten-thirty a.m.?

Huh?

The only good thing about all this stuff going on is I'm not thinking about the MUSIC FESTIVAL as much. (Just a little...)

Now that ALL the **TICKETS** are SOLD my only chance of going is WINNING the **FREE TICKET DRAW** that Dad said he entered.

Yes!

I'm putting on a BRAVE face and Derek is doing a good job of making me laugh.

Tom ... how do you make a sausage roll?

I don't know.

Push it down a hill.

(Nice one...)

I'm hoping that after lunch Marcus will be in a better mood, although he still looks a bit cross.

I tell him Derek's sausage roll joke and he's trying not to laugh. (I can tell.)

Miss Gravel announces she has the list of who's playing what in the school play.

"Please let me be the GIANT," Marcus mumbles over and over again.

If you get a MAIN part, there's quite a lot of rehearsing to do, so I'd rather avoid that.
I wouldn't even mind being a tree again.

Miss Gravel wants us all to be QUIET before she hands out the cast list.
Norman does a bit of chair **SCRAPING,**

Whoops...

"AAAAPE

so she keeps us all waiting even longer.

There's lots of shushing

going on from around the class,

until finally ...

SILENCE.

She hands out the forms, and from the look on Marcus's FACE, I'm guessing he didn't get to be the GIANT.

WHAT?

tom

There's a list pinned on the school NOTICEBOARD as well.

JACK AND THE BEANSTALK
School Play

Jack ———————— Tracey, 5N
Giant ———————— Solid, 5F
Mother ———————— Lucy, 5N
Cow ———————— Front/Back
Norman 5F/Derek, 5S
Monster ———————— Tom, 5F
Farmer ———————— John, 4P
Farmer ———————— Amy, 5F
Farmer ———————— Harry, 4B
Farmer ———————— Cheryl, 5S

BEANSTALKS ——— Marcus, 5F/
Everyone else in the Red
Group
Villagers ——— Blue Group
Market
stallholders ——— Yellow Group

It's here

STAGE HELPERS needed too!

PLAY Auditions

SM**ALL**^{CABB}**AGES**

WELCOME!

I had no idea there was a **MONSTER** in JACK and the BEANSTALK. Miss Gravel explains that I'm going to be popping up in different scenes so the audience can SPOT me and shout,

It's the **MONSTER!**

"I'm sure it will be fine, Tom. If I was doing the play it might be different, but I'm not going to be here much longer," she adds in a slightly disapproving way.

AMY seems happy about being a farmer.

Unlike Marcus...

Who's not happy at all.

A beanstalk! I don't look like a beanstalk. Do I?

"**N**ot yet, but we did make a lot of leaves,

so you will soon," I tell him.

Derek and **N**orman are two halves of the COW.

Norman is already KEEN to have a practice.

As soon as the BELL goes for home, we push in our

chairs. (In s i l e n c e .)

Norman finds **D**erek so they can try out

some COW moves walking home.

If this is anything to go by,

I think JACK AND THE BEANSTALK

is going to be very funny.

On the back of our forms there's more information about what costumes we'll need to wear.

Mine just says MONSTER – wear something that looks like a monster. Which is not very helpful but I have a few ideas.

Norman and Derek have done COW-walking all the way to the shop, where we stop to read the **NEWSPAPER** sign.

OAKFIELD GAZETTE

NO MORE TICKETS LEFT AT ALL FOR OAKCHELLA! LAST FREE TICKET DRAW DONE

 "Good job I've got my ticket already,"

Norman says.

"Yeah ... isn't it,"

I sigh.

When I get home I go straight to see Dad, who's in his shed working.

I want to ask him if we've WON the **tickets,** and tell him what part I've got in the school play. (Also, he might have wafers.)

I *BURST* through the door and "SURPRISE" him. "Dad, guess what? I'm a **MONSTER!"** I shout, which makes him SPIN round in his chair.

"Yes, you are, Tom! Definitely a **MONSTER!"**

"No, Dad, I'm a **MONSTER** in the PLAY – that's my part. Did we win the last FESTIVAL **tickets?"** I want to know.

"No news yet, and isn't the play JACK and the BEANSTALK?"

"It IS!" I show Dad the school play form, which explains more.

"Ahhh, so you're a funny **MONSTER** that randomly appears in different scenes?"

"EXACTLY - and I have to make a costume too. Something like THIS." 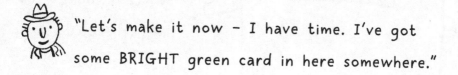 I show him my **MONSTER** doodle.

"Let's make it now - I have time. I've got some BRIGHT green card in here somewhere."

"Have you got WAFERS too?" I ask hopefully.

"Go on - but just take one," Dad says and points to a tin that's not very well hidden.

(Making **MONSTERS** is hungry work...)

With Dad's help, it doesn't take long to cut out the card and make a really good costume.

"You might need to wear some green trousers," Dad tells me when I try it on.

I want to see what it looks like, so I go back into the house ...

... and bump into Delia.

"This is my school play **MONSTER** costume,  in case you're wondering," I tell her before she can say anything.

"Why bother? You don't need a costume, Tom," she says, so I ignore her and take a look in the hall mirror.

"I think it looks GREAT," I say. Then I take it off and go into the kitchen.

"AGHHH! It's HORRIBLE!"
Delia shouts, pretending to be SCARED of me.

"Ha! Ha! Very funny," I sigh.

 "Are you looking forward to seeing the cousins this weekend?" she asks me.

(I remember she's going to the FESTIVAL this weekend and I'm not.)

"Yes I am, actually.

It's going to be FANTASTIC.

Aunty Alice and Uncle Kevin have got something

really special planned for us. It's probably going

to be BETTER than the FESTIVAL," I tell Delia,

pretending to be more enthusiastic than I am.

"Well, I know where I'd rather be,"

Delia says.

(Me too. She had to

remind me...)

Miss Gravel's
last day...

The GOOD NEWS is that it's
Miss Gravel's last day. You'd think she'd be
HAPPY. (I know I am.) But she looks FuRIOuS.

"I'm sorry, Class 5F. I've had a very difficult morning RUNNING around
LOOKING for my missing dog."

BANDIT!   I shout because I
           know his name.

"That's right, Tom — Bandit."

"Did you find him, Miss Gravel?" AMY asks.

"I did. He was trying to ESCAPE into the neighbour's garden
and got STUCK!"

 "Poor **BANDIT**," I say.

"He's fine," Miss Gravel tells us.

As I've lugged my **MONSTER** costume into
school today, I'm hoping to leave it here.
I don't want to take it back home as well.

Miss Gravel spots my costume and suggests I put
it somewhere safe.

 "We don't want anything happening to it in class, Tom.
If you go quickly, Mrs Nap's in the hall right now.
No dawdling, though."

Yes, Miss Gravel, I say.

Marcus even says he likes my costume.

Being a
MONSTER
suits you, Tom.

(Sort of.)

It's a chance to get out of lessons, so I'm keen to go *FAST.*

I wear the **MONSTER** all the way down the hall, surprising some little kids on the way.

Mrs Nap sees me and she JUMPS as well. "You gave me a SCARE, Tom – but I love the **MONSTER** costume!" Then she adds, "I think this is going to be a WONDERFUL addition to Jack and the Beanstalk – well done!"

Which is nice to hear.

Mrs Nap asks me to put my costume with all the other ones on the stage behind the curtain.

I can see all kinds of interesting-looking props as well...

I look for a safe place to put it and settle for resting it against a chair so it doesn't fall down.

I RESIST the chance to try on any of the props or silly hats as Miss Gravel told me to come straight back.

... Almost.

Mrs **N**ap catches me messing around and tells me to go back to class.

"Miss Gravel has booked the hall for your class this afternoon," she says.

(Which doesn't sound like something

Miss **G**ravel would do.)

 "It's her last day, Tom — I think she might be planning something fun for the whole class," **M**rs **N**ap tells me.

I'm not so sure.

(I think that — I don't say it aloud.)

As most of us are having school dinners today there's no more missing-food drama, which is good. 🙂 ALTHOUGH Marcus did SPOT the 🐍 SNAKE I drew on the wall.

"A SNAKE didn't eat my sausage roll, Tom," he wants me to know.

"It was kind of a joke, Marcus," I say. There's a lot of chat about WHO'S going to OAKCHELLA, ♫ ♫ which is just what I want to hear.

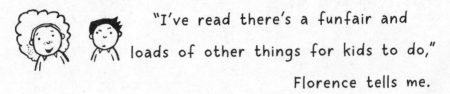

"I've read there's a funfair and loads of other things for kids to do," Florence tells me.

"Oh, great," I sigh.

"There'll probably be ice cream and candyfloss too," Norman joins in.

"Tom's not going, are you, Tom?" Marcus reminds everyone.

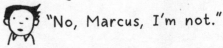 "No, Marcus, I'm not."

"**L**ots of kids aren't going. Anyway, I'll be at my cousins and we're doing something **AMAZING**," I tell him — which is a mistake.

"Like what?" he asks.

"Um, I'm not sure yet. It's a SURPRISE," I say.

Derek helps me out. "The **FESTIVAL** might not EVEN be that good. We don't know yet."

AMY agrees. "I've heard it's going to rain too, so it could be **MUDDY**."

I can tell they're BOTH trying to make me feel better, so I say, "I'm sure you'll all have a fantastic time."

"I KNOW I WILL!"
Marcus shouts, then he dances around when he really doesn't have to.

Back in class it turns out that Miss Gravel ACTuALLY HAS planned for us to play games in the hall this afternoon ...

... which is unexpected.

Caretaker Stan is in there working on the stage lights, turning them ON and OFF quite a lot.

"I won't be long," he tells Miss Gravel, as we file into the hall.

"That's OK, Stan. Please carry on," she tells him, then stands on the stage to make an announcement.

"You've all worked EXCEPTIONALLY hard this week so I thought you'd ENJOY letting off a bit of STEAM."

(I have to ask  what that means.)

"Having fun, relaxing," she whispers.

"Oh," I say, as that's not something you'd expect to hear from Miss Gravel.

"I know some of you thought I was a bit ... STRICT. I just like to get things done QUICKLY and QUIETLY. So well done, everyone. You see, I'm NOT SCARY AT ALL!"

Which would have been easier to believe if Caretaker Stan hadn't turned on some BRIGHT lights that made everyone GASP!

HUUUUUUUUUUUUUH?

(Uh-oh! I recognize that monster. So I keep quiet.)

"Is everything OK, Class 5F?" Miss Gravel asks us.

"There's something behind you!"
Brad Galloway tells her.

Miss Gravel looks EXTRA fierce until Stan turns the lights off.

Which is a BIG relief for me.

(At least I know my costume
kind of works though.)

Last night, Mum was grumbling about going
to her WORK DO at the weekend.
She EVEN said, "It's a shame we didn't get tickets
for the FESTIVAL, isn't it?"

Awww, Mum!

Which was annoying.

Dad told her they didn't HAVE to go to the
WORK DO. "As the kids are both out, we could
always do something else?"

"We could go to a garden centre?"
Mum suggested. (Which sounds terrible.
I'm glad I'm going to the cousins.)
Even though it's raining this morning, Delia is keen
to get out the door.

I'm OFF, she shouts, before Mum and
Dad can ask any more
questions about the
FESTIVAL.

I'm ready too. All my essentials are packed.

Sock puppet - useful for annoying the cousins

My painted rock collection

Notebook

Pens

One pair of socks

Snacks

Pyjamas

Toothbrush so I don't end up like Granddad (no teeth)

I bring my bag downstairs and I can hear Mum on the phone. I can tell it's someone from work as she has her **"WORK VOICE"** on. Mum's COUGHING a lot and sounds a bit ill. Then she puts the phone down and comes to see me.

 "Morning, Tom. Have you got everything ready?" Mum asks, not COUGHING at all.

"Yes! When are we leaving?" I want to know.

"Soon. I've just got to find the tent."

"Are you camping? For work? You hate camping!"

I say, which is TRUE.

"Errr ... we might be doing something

else now..." Mum tells me.

"OK," I say.

Then Dad comes down and starts

putting things in the car.

"Are you all set, Tom?" he asks, taking

my bag. "What have you got here? It

feels heavy..."

"Only important things I need,"

I tell him as we have a quick breakfast.

"Are you looking forward to camping?"

I ask, suspiciously.

Before he can answer, Mum asks us "Shall

we get going, then?" like she's forgotten **ALL**

about being so grumpy.

In the car, Dad keeps saying he hopes it stops raining.

"Hmmmm," I sigh, looking at the clouds.
"Me too."

We pull up at the cousins' house and WEIRDLY everyone is outside waiting for us.

Aunty Alice and my cousins are waving while Uncle Kevin is telling us where to park.

"Are we late?" Mum wonders.

"I don't think so..." Dad replies.

"Crikey, Frank, is that rust-bucket still going? Glad you made it," is the first thing Uncle Kevin says.

"Great to see you too." Dad smiles and gets out of the car.

"Thanks for having Tom," Mum says.

I jump out of the car and try to drag my bag in.

"Are you here for the WEEK, Tom? That looks HEAVY," Uncle Kevin says.

"Just essentials," I say.

We get out of the rain and go inside.

I notice everyone has on welly boots and Uncle Kevin is looking very colourful.

"Nice shirt, Kevin," Dad tells him.

"Where are you off to then?" Mum wonders.

"We have a surprise for you, Tom," Aunty Alice says, which sounds interesting.

"Are we going to *Chocolate World?*" I ask, as I've always wanted to go there.

"I'm afraid not. Hopefully you'll think this is better than that..."

(I'm trying to not look disappointed.)

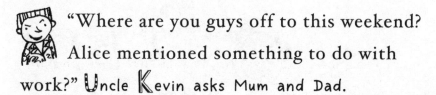
"Where are you guys off to this weekend? Alice mentioned something to do with work?" Uncle Kevin asks Mum and Dad.

"We've had a small change of plan," Mum says.

"It's great Tom can spend time with you," Dad adds.

I'm still waiting to hear what my surprise is.

"Well I don't think Tom will be disappointed..." Uncle Kevin says.

(I might be.)

"Because of my connections, I've managed to get us FIVE tickets to OAKCHELLA Festival with special VIP access too!"

"Are you excited, Tom?"

Aunty Alice asks me...

YES!
I AM!

"Oh really? That's great,"
Mum and Dad say. But not in
a very enthusiastic way.

"Won't Tom need boots and stuff?"
Mum wants to know.

 "We can lend him everything he needs, even a waterproof coat," Aunty Alice assures Mum.

"Great! I don't want to have to wear a bin
liner again," I chip in, remembering all the
times I've done that.

 "Why on EARTH would you wear a bin
liner, Tom?" Uncle Kevin asks me.

"Bin liners can be very useful in an EMERGENCY," Dad tells him.

I'm so happy to be going, I high-five the cousins. Mum and Dad tell me to be good and have a great time and that they'll pick me up late tomorrow.

"The BEST PART of these tickets is they give us a pass for both days so we're coming home to sleep in our nice warm beds," Uncle Kevin adds.

"No camping then? Lucky you," Mum sighs.

"Camping is all part of the FESTIVAL experience," Dad says.

"Not for us it's not. It's such a shame you're not coming. It would've been great for us all to be there ... together," Uncle Kevin says.

"We'll be with you in spirit,"
Dad tells him.

"Yes, closer than you think," Mum adds.

"T his is better than *Chocolate World!*"
I say, then wave BYE to Mum
and Dad as they head OFF.

I'm going to
OAKCHELLA FESTIVAL
after all! YIPPEE!

I can't believe that.

What are we going to do?

GO! But keep out of their way.

Yes!

Hide?

When we get to OAKCHELLA, we all have to wear
special wristbands and I have my very own **VIP**
pass to wear around my neck. Uncle Kevin is very
pleased our passes get us into the
"right" places.

And Florence was right! There are loads
of other things to do as well.

In our special section, we have a BRILLIANT VIEW of the stage and there's a place where you can go and just HELP YOURSELF to FOOD! It's useful when there's a band on we don't like.

The cousins and I go out to look around the festival and **BUMP** into a bunch of my friends – who are all pleased (and SURPRISED!) to see me, as I said I wasn't coming.

Delia's not so pleased. (I've never seen her dance like that before.)

If Mum and Dad were here they'd love it too. I can't wait to tell them all about it.

I'm keeping my wristband
on so everyone can see
I went to the FESTIVAL.

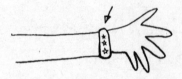

Mr Fullerman is BACK and we're all so HAPPY
to see him. ☺

Hello, Class 5F!
How was Miss Gravel?
Did you have
a good time?

S I L E N C E

(There is a little bit of mumbling around the class.)

"**S**he was quite strict, sir," I tell him.

"She did let us play games on her last day though," **AMY** adds, which is true.

 **"It doesn't sound like you had too bad a week to me!"** Mr Fullerman tells us.

Straight away, Marcus lets Mr Fullerman know about his "MISSING SAUSAGE ROLLS!"

Then Mark Clump puts HIS hand up and says he thinks it's an ANIMAL of some kind stealing food.

It's a SNAKE! Brad Galloway shouts out.

 **"Really? I've missed so much. It sounds very exciting and like you'll all be GLAD to get back to doing some work."**

(We all groan a little.)

It does feel like things are back to normal again
now that Mr Fullerman's here.

He even lets us CHAT about the FESTIVAL.
It's brilliant that I can actually join in AND show
off my wristband.

Marcus just wants to talk about his packed lunch.
"Today I've got a Cornish pasty* and it's delicious,"
he says, licking his lips.

"Do you think it'll still be there at lunchtime?"
I ask.

"Yes, Tom. Now Mr Fullerman's back, I don't think
anyone will steal my food," Marcus says, confidently.

*A Cornish pasty is like a pie shaped like this➔ and filled with veg and meat.

When **Mr Fullerman** asks for
volunteers to take some files
down to the school office, everyone's keen to help.
My hand shoots up fast, so he picks me and **AMY**.

"Don't be too long," he tells us.

"Yes, sir."

We're walking down to the office when **AMY**
notices a line of crumbs on the floor. They go all
the way down the hall ... and STOP right outside
the STOCK ROOM door, which is slightly open.

AMY and I look at each other.

"Shall we go in and see what it
is?" I say.

Amy isn't sure. "We're not allowed in the stock
room. We could get in trouble," she tells me.

"I know, but there's SOMETHING in there. We should SEE what it is."

"What if it's a SNAKE?" AMY asks.

 "It won't be," I say. (But I hadn't thought of that.) "Let's just take a quick look anyway."

We're just about to open the door when Caretaker Stan gives us a ⋛SHOCK.⋚

"Where do you two think you're going?" he wants to know.

"There's SOMETHING in the stock room," I try and explain. "Look! The door's open!"

"Listen!" AMY says. We can hear popping noises.

"OK — you two stay here and I'll take a look." We wait outside as Caretaker Stan OPENS the door. And inside ...

IT'S BANDIT!

He's sitting on a piece of bubble
wrap and EATING what looks like
Marcus's Cornish pasty.

That's Miss Gravel's dog!" I tell Caretaker Stan.

"Well, she'll have to come and pick him up.
Cheeky dog! I wonder if he's been the one
stealing all the food..." he asks.

"Maybe that's why he's called **Bandit!**"
AMY says.
I hadn't thought of that.
We stay and play with **Bandit** while Caretaker Stan
goes to the school office with our files - and to
call Miss Gravel.

We're a bit late getting back to class, but we
have a **VERY** good excuse.

We don't see **Bandit** again until the school play.

Miss Gravel brings him with her to watch us. She's like a different person when she's not being our teacher. Very SMILEY and she doesn't seem strict at all.

Bandit is VERY well behaved and sits quietly on Miss Gravel's lap for the WHOLE play.

Being a monster in the play is the BEST part EVER as I don't have to learn any lines and everyone laughs and enjoys it whenever I come on stage.

I think my **MONSTER** costume has worked out really well. Derek and Norman are a big hit as the cow too.

And Marcus ...

... makes an EXCELLENT beanstalk.

There are <u>SO</u> many reasons to get the paper today.

Delia's bought the paper today which is handy.
I'm taking a good look at the photos of the
FESTIVAL (before she catches me).

I'm trying to see if I can spot myself in the
BIG photo.

I can see Delia, and Marcus...

There's ME! And the cousins!

I even spot Mr Fullerman.

I find Santa Claus, an alien, a snake (ha!),
a panda, a cat...

There's so much to see.

HANG ON a second...

Is that?

There are two people right at
the top that look a bit like ...
Mum and Dad?

That can't be right, can it?

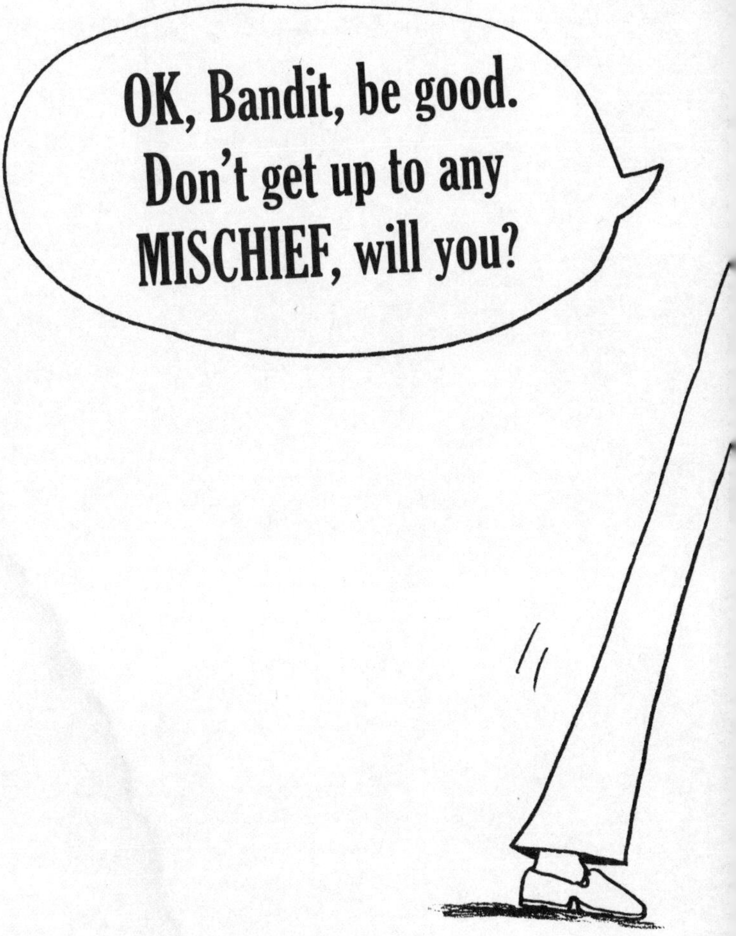
OK, Bandit, be good. Don't get up to any MISCHIEF, will you?

Bandit

Rules of Champ

(It's also called Four Square.)

① **U**se your hand to hit the ball (no scooping).

② **O**nly **one** ❍ bounce allowed but the ⬇ ball can go to any of the four squares.

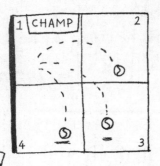

To BECOME the

CHAMP you move around the squares. **B**ut if you're **OUT** you go to the back of the queue, <u>or</u> to square **four** if there's no one waiting.

You must try to stay in CHAMP SQUARE
for as long as possible to become the

(Oh yes!)

Tom Gates' Glossary

(Which means explanations for stuff
that might sound a bit ODD.)

A **bin liner** is a garbage bag.

Earwigging means eavesdropping.

 is the attendance book that the
teacher would ✓ tick you off in
in the morning to make sure
you're not LATE.

Caramel wafers: 'Excellent' biscuits (cookies)
⬆ covered in
chocolate with layers of
caramel and wafer inside.

Welly Boots are rubber boots.

When Liz ⬛ was little ∩, she loved to draw, paint and make things. Her mum used to say she was very good at making a mess (which is still true today!).

She kept drawing and went to art school, where she earned a degree in graphic design. She worked as a designer and art director in the music industry 🎸, and her freelance work has appeared on a wide variety of products.

Liz is the author-illustrator of several picture books. Tom Gates is the first series of books she has written and illustrated for older children. They have won several prestigious awards ⭐, including the Roald Dahl Funny Prize, the Waterstones Children's Book Prize, and the Blue Peter Book Award. The books have been translated into forty-three languages worldwide.

Visit her at www.LizPichon.com

OAKFIELD GAZETTE

BREAKING NEWS

MORE TOM GATES BOOKS TO ADD TO YOUR COLLECTION

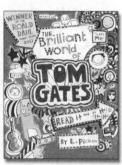

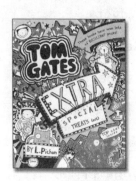

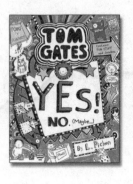

So many

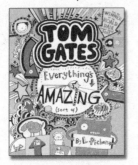

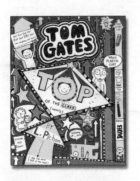

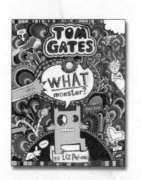

New Book